Everything Belongs to the Future

Everything Belongs to the Future

EVERYTHING BELONGS TO THE FUTURE

LAURIE PENNY

A TOM DOHERTY ASSOCIATES BOOK

NEW YORK

EVERYTHING BELONGS TO THE FUTURE

Copyright © 2016 by Laurie Penny

Cover photograph by Oleksiy Maksymenko/Getty Images
Cover design by FORT

Edited by Patrick Nielsen Hayden

A Tor.com Book
Published by Tom Doherty Associates
175 Fifth Avenue
New York, NY 10010

www.tor.com

Tor® is a registered trademark of Macmillan Publishing Group, LLC.

ISBN 978-0-7653-8827-8 (ebook)
ISBN 978-0-7653-8828-5 (trade paperback)

First Edition: October 2016

For Magpie

Everything Belongs to the Future

Everything Belongs to the Future

Dear Daisy,

We were never really friends, were we? Somehow, though, you're the person I want to write to most in here. I hope these letters get to you. I'm giving them to Alex, who I am absolutely sure is reading them too, and although they aren't meant for him, I hope he gets something instructive from them.

Hello, Alex. I hope you're well. I hope you're safe. I hope you understand that you are not forgiven. Even after the awful, terrible thing we did. Even after the Time Bomb, and everything that came afterward. I can't let it go. The anger keeps me sharp. Keeps my brain from turning to paste. It's that or the crossword, and rage is more reliable. I am sorry about your hands, though.

Anyway. I've got a story for you, this time. For both of you, as it happens.

Have you heard the one about the Devil's bridge?

It's an old story, and there are lots of different tellings, but it goes something like this.

A carpenter wants to build a bridge across a river. Not just any bridge, but the strongest, sturdiest bridge that has ever been made or thought of, to take him and his wife to the far bank, where there are treasures whose nature is unimportant to the story. Let us assume that he has good reasons for wanting to get there, or thinks he does. Let us assume that his tools and skills are insufficient to the task. Let us assume that he is out of options and ideas.

He sits down on the plain, gray bank he calls home and makes a wish.

Instantly there appears before him a handsome man with savage eyes and shining hair, and his clothes are rich and strange and he blinks less than a person ought to, and the carpenter knows that this is the Devil.

I can build a bridge for you, says the Devil. I can build you a bridge across the wild, wide river, and it will be the greatest bridge ever seen, the strongest, the most magnificent. It will stand for a hundred years, and people from all around will come to walk on it and say: the man who made this must be a fine carpenter indeed. The bridge will draw visitors from seven counties. Boys will take their sweethearts here to propose. You can charge an entry fee. You can open a hot-dog stand. Whatever you want.

I'm not really interested in that, says the carpenter. I just want to get to the other side.

Well, says the Devil, that's part of the package.

What would it cost me? says the carpenter.

Alright, I don't have a lot of time left to write. They come in and stop me at guard change.

Meanwhile: consider that time is a weapon.

Before the coming of the Time Bomb, this was true. It was true before men and women of means or special merit could purchase an extra century of youth. It has been true since the invention of the hour-glass, the water clock, the wristwatch, the shift-bell, the factory floor. Ever since men could measure time, they have used it to divide each other.

Time is a weapon wielded by the rich, who have excess of it, against the rest, who must trade every breath of it against the promise of another day's food and shelter. What kind of world have we made, where human beings can live centuries if only they can afford the fix? What kind of creatures have we become?

The Time Bomb. Aerosolized gerontoxin. Currently being deployed around a world in panic by desperate people with nothing to lose and nothing to make but their point. You know you could have *stopped it. Alex, I'm talking to you now. You could have stopped it all from happening. Maybe someday soon I'll tell them how. After all, so much life has been wasted.*

So very much life.

. . .

There was a wall. It was taller than it seemed and set back a little from the street, so the ancient trees on the college side provided a well of darker shadow, away from the streetlights.

The wall was old and rough, ancient sandstone filled in with reinforced cement to keep out intruders. The drop on the other side landed you in thick grass. Still, Alex was afraid of the wall. Of the idea of it.

Nina was the first to make the climb. She squatted on top of the wall, an implike thing in the darkness. Then she turned and held out her hand to Alex, beckoning.

"You have to see this," she said.

Alex started to climb the wall between the worlds. The old stone bit at his hands. Halfway up, he heard Nina make a little sound of disappointment in her throat. He was never fast enough for her.

The approach to Magdalen College was across the deer park.

That was where they were going: through the park, avoiding the dogs and the security lights, into the college, into the ball all sparkling under the starlight.

It was four of them, Nina and Alex, Margo and Fidget, and they were off to rob the rich and feed the poor. An exercise, as Margo put it, as important for the emotional welfare of the autonomous individual as it was for the collective. Margo was a state therapist before she came to Cowley, to bunker down with the rest of the strays and degenerates clinging to the underside of Oxford city. Five years of living off the grid hadn't cured her of the talk.

At the top of the wall, Alex unfolded himself for an instant, and then he saw it—what Nina had been trying to show him. The old college lit from behind with a hundred moving lights, butter-soft and pink and pretty, a bubble of beauty floating on the skin of time.

"It's beautiful," he said.

"Come on," said Margo, "get moving, or we'll be seen."

Margo was beside him now, the great bulk of her making no sound on the ascent. Alex's mouth had been dry all night. He licked his teeth and listened to his heart shake the bars of his rib cage. He had promised the others that he was good for this. He wasn't going to have another anxiety attack and ruin everything.

"As your therapist," said Margo, gentling her voice, "I should remind you that God hates a coward."

Alex jumped before she could push him, and hit the grass on the other side of the wall without remembering to bend his knees. His ankles cried out on impact.

Then Nina was next to him, and Margo, all three of them together. Fidget was last, dropping over the wall without a sound, dark on dark in the moonlight. Margo held up a hand for assembly.

"Security's not going to be tight on this side of the college. Let's go over the drill if anyone gets caught."

"We're the hired entertainment and our passes got lost somewhere," said Nina, stripping off her coverall. Underneath, she was wearing a series of intricately knotted bedsheets, and the overall effect was somewhere between appropriative and indecent.

Alex liked it.

"Alex," said Margo, "I want to hear it from you. What are you?"

"I'm a stupid drunk entertainer and I'm not being paid enough for this," Alex repeated.

"Good. Now, as your therapist, I advise you to run very fast, meet us at the fountain, take nothing except what we came for, and for fuck's sake, don't get caught."

Fireworks bloomed and snickered in the sky over the deer park. Chill fingers of light and laughter uncurled from the ancient college. They moved off separately across the dark field to the perimeter.

Alex squinted to make out the deer, but the herd was elsewhere, sheltering from the revelry. The last wild deer in England. Oxford guarded its treasures, flesh and stone both.

Alex kept low, and he had almost made it to the wall when a searchlight swung around, pinning him there.

Alex was an insect frozen against the sandstone.

Alex couldn't remember who he was supposed to be.

Alex was about to fuck this up for everyone and get them all sent to jail before they'd even got what they came for.

Hands on Alex's neck, soft, desperate, and a small firm body pinning him against the wall. Fidget. Fidget, kissing him sloppily, fumbling with the buttons on his shirt, both of them caught in the beam of light.

"Play along," Fidget hissed, and Alex understood. He groaned theatrically as Fidget ran hard hands through his hair and kissed his open mouth. Alex had never kissed another man like this before, and he was too shit-scared to wonder whether he liked it, because if they couldn't convince whoever was on the other end of that searchlight that they were a couple of drunks who'd left the party to fuck, they were both going to jail.

The searchlight lingered.

Fidget ran a sharp, scoundrel tongue along Alex's neck. A spike of anger stabbed Alex in the base of his belly, but instead of punching Fidget in his pretty face, he grabbed his head, twisted it up and kissed him again.

The searchlight lingered, trembling.

Fidget fumbled with Alex's belt buckle.

The searchlight moved on.

Fidget sighed in the merciful darkness. "I thought I was going to have to escalate for a second there."

"You seemed to be having a good time," said Alex.

"Don't flatter yourself," said Fidget. "The word you're looking for is 'thanks.'"

They were almost inside. Just behind the last fence, Magdalen ball was blossoming into being. Behind the fence, airy music from somewhere out of time would be rising over the lacquered heads of five hundred guests in suits and rented ballgowns. Entertainers and waitstaff in themed costumes would be circling with trays of champagne flutes. Chocolates and cocaine would be laid out in intricate lines on silver dishes.

Alex and the others weren't here for any of that.

They were here for the fix.

• • •

Daisy Craver had come to this party under protest. Her company liked to show her off at events like these, just another expensive decoration in this stage-managed whirl of decadence they were sponsoring. That's what Daisy was to them—a prestige piece. No different from the biosculptures in the lobby at the lab. She hadn't done any real work in years.

Instead, she got wheeled out to these things like an angry puppet to pick at ridiculous miniature food and talk to brainless, braying rich kids and their parents, who were all just so grateful for her research. At least, the parents were. The kids probably hated her—sure, they got to be young and healthy for an extra half-century, but Mummy and Daddy got that same half-century to spend the inheritance. Without that, they were having to find other ways to maintain the lifestyles to which they had become accustomed.

"It'll be good for you." That's what Parker had said. Parker was Daisy's supervisor, although she thought of him as her handler. What he meant was "it'll be good for us." The work she had done back in the twenties was essential to the base formula of the fix, and that made her essential to the company. An important resource, they said. Like all the other geniuses who got the life-extension grants.

Daisy didn't take it as a compliment. She knew what multinationals did with important resources.

Still, she put on the stupid frock with the ruffles that neither suited nor fit her and got in the limo, and now she was hanging around the fountain, eating chocolate-covered marshmallows and trying to avoid the undergraduates in their prom gowns and penguin suits. Parker wanted her to show her face. He never specified that there should be a smile on it.

Daisy hated parties, and this one was particularly hateful, a shaken snow globe of opulence just begging to be dashed on the floor. The theme was "The Fountain of Youth." It was based on a weird old racist novel where some British explorers went to darkest Africa and discovered a tribe of savages ruled by an immortal queen who was for some reason as white as they were.

The theme had been chosen in honor of the sponsor, Daisy's own company, TeamThreeHundred, which held the patent for the broadest-spectrum life-extension drugs on the market. The distinctive little blue pills went for two hundred dollars a pop on the black market—less if you could afford the right insurance. One pill a day, every day, was enough to keep your meat fresh for decades and more. There were people who'd started to fix fifty years before who hadn't counted a single gray hair.

Rich people, mostly, and anyone deemed socially useful enough that their continued existence was worth sponsoring, although that too was up to the manufacturers to decide. Artists, musicians, scientists. Even the occasional writer. Meritocracy in action.

Daisy had never liked parties, though—even when she was young, really young, not just young-looking. Not that she ever got invited to many parties back in school. Not that she had cared. More time to spend on the net, talking to professors three times her age about gene splicing.

Daisy had been born at the turn of this millennium, on the exact day that the completion of the Human Genome Project had been announced to the world. She had seen it in the old stills—the government scientist and the venture capitalist standing on either side of the president at the time, one of the Clintons or one of the Bushes, all their differences buried in public, a new dawn for the future of biotech.

None of these kids necking free cocktails would remember. Even the ones who were already fixing—and Daisy could tell, she could always tell; there was an uncanny smoothness to the skin, a ghastly glisten that made them doll-like. They wouldn't be old enough to remember a time when money could only buy, at best, the appearance of youth.

The fountain was the centerpiece. The old stone sprinkler with its constipated-looking cherubs had been decked out as the Fountain of Youth, but it was only running cheap champagne, cut with Prosecco.

It was the little dishes around the side that held the

real juice. Candy bowls of blue pills. Fashioned like arrows, more precious than diamonds. The fix. Free to those who could afford it, courtesy of our generous sponsors.

Daisy was alone.

These days, she was always alone.

She opened her tablet and called up an old video. Scrubbed from the net now, but she had a copy. Pixelated, seventy years old, but the sound was clear.

A dark stage. A quiet audience of professionals. A single podium, and there she was—a much younger, identical-looking Daisy, giving one of the last unscripted ethics talks she had ever got away with.

"The mold strain Aspergillus aevitas *is native to Orkney in the Republic of Scotland. Since its discovery and cultivation by my department, the Future of Humanity Institute at Oxford, and following development by TeamThreeHundred, this fungus has made the dream of significantly extending not just human life but human youth a reality.*

"Thank you. In the course of my research for the company, completed with my coauthor Doctor Saladin Hasan, I was an early recipient of TeamThreeHundred's extension program. At forty years old, I have the vital statistics of a person less than half my age. With regular treatment, I can expect to live well into the next century without any deterioration in quality of life."

Applause from the audience, most of whom, Daisy reflected, would be long dead by now, except those with company health plans.

"*Thank you. I hope that these extra years of useful work will be as much of an asset to the department and the company that sponsored this groundbreaking research as they will be of personal benefit to me. You've heard from people far higher up in the company how those who are now receiving the second generation of extension treatments can expect to live some three centuries, barring accidents and acts of God. You still need to look both ways before you cross the road. Ahaha. Yes. That's the line we're all using today. How did I do?*

"*Anyway, it remains to be seen what the effects of this miraculous technology will be on the world our grandchildren inherit—although perhaps I shouldn't use the word 'inherit,' since I fully intend to be around to see it myself.*"

More applause from the audience of ghosts.

"*Thank you. I'm here today as a technologist, but also as a scholar of the history of science. History shows us that the ramifications of any new technology have as much to do with how we choose to distribute it as they have to do with the technology itself. I am not a politician, nor am I an economist. I am a scientist. But it seems appropriate to hypothesize here that a future where life-extension technology is available only to those who can afford it, or to those whom society con-*

*siders useful, will look very different to a future where life-ex-
tension technology is more broadly available. I'm sorry—*

"I'm sorry, something seems to have gone wrong with the
sound . . ."

A noise behind Daisy. Parker Tremaine walked heavily
across the damp grass, carrying two glasses of champagne. Knowing Parker, it'd be the good stuff.

She darkened her tablet quickly, and the ghost of her
younger self disappeared, too late for him to miss. Aside
from being the closest she still had to a direct boss,
Parker was the one person in the entire company who
had been been fixed for as long as she had, back when he
was an entrepreneurial prodigy in the early days of T3, in
what later became the Free State of California.

They knew each other too well for her to hide things
from him.

"Memory lane?" he asked. He still had the lazy West-
Coast accent. "Here. I brought us some bubbly. We're
due a chat, you and me."

"No, thanks." Daisy patted her hip flask. "Whisky
only."

"Suit yourself. More for me." Parker downed one glass
in a single fizzy swig and tossed it away over the lawn. He
was already drunk.

They looked out together over the college lawns, toward the hills of Headington. A small forest of turbines

churned away on the horizon. There were hardly any in the old city.

"It's amazing, when you think about how it used to be," said Parker quietly.

Daisy took a swig. "Not going to argue with you on that."

It was always somebody else's apocalypse. Until it wasn't.

The end of the world was an endless dark tomorrow: always arriving but never actually here. For generations, the elected and unelected leaders of the world had weighed the cost of averting drastic climate change via collective, immediate and lasting technological investment against the considerable inconvenience to their personal lifestyles, done some calculations on the back of a napkin and come up with the answer that it was somebody else's problem. Somebody who probably hadn't been born yet. If all else failed, their own children and grandchildren would probably be able to afford a place on the last helicopter out of the drowning lands. So, that was alright.

The fix changed everything.

Suddenly, the same people had to plan for a future in which they'd actually be around to see London and New York swallowed by the hungry ocean. Suddenly, the end of the world was a story about them.

The solutions came fast. But not fast enough to save Bangladesh. Or Venice. Or San Francisco.

"In all the world, we're the only two creatures quite like us," said Parker after a while. He lifted his second glass of champagne and looked at Daisy. "Remind me again why we've never fucked?"

"That's easy," said Daisy. "It's because I don't fancy you."

For an instant, a flicker of real, childlike anger chased across Parker's cherub face, and was gone. He ran his fingers through his perfect blond hair and smiled.

"Ever considered lesbianism?"

"Thoroughly. And regularly. You know I prefer dicks when they're attached to women."

This was a complete and utter lie. Daisy had not had sex in ten years. Daisy had not had fun of any kind since she could remember, but particularly not horizontal fun involving other humans. Keeping her appearance static at awkward mid-puberty helped with that. It was one of the few decisions she'd never regretted. Plenty of people might like the idea of an eternal fourteen-year-old, but they changed their tune when they met her, all gangly limbs and acne scars and flashes of anger.

A long time ago, there had been someone who'd seen past her defenses. Someone who'd made her feel that she was more than a brain trapped in a twist of preserved flesh, a specimen suspended in amber. Someone who had loved her—actively, he always said, because love is not something you feel but something you do.

But he had been dead these forty years.

Daisy picked at her fingernail and glared at Parker.

"Actually," she said, "speaking of dicks attached to women, where's your better half? Lila, wasn't it? I liked her. She was funny."

Parker went quiet.

"We had different life goals," he said eventually.

"She wouldn't fix, would she?"

Parker's expression twisted and flushed. There was something truly unnerving, Daisy thought, about watching extremely good-looking people trying not to cry, like seeing a beautiful painting slashed and torn.

"Bitch," said Parker.

He took a deep breath and put his face back into his champagne. Daisy swigged from her hip flask.

"I know what you're up to," he said quietly.

"If you did, you wouldn't say so," she said.

"You want to be careful," he said. "You haven't got many friends in this company, you know. If it wasn't for my vouching for you—"

"I haven't got any friends in this company," said Daisy. "'Friend' is not the correct word for what you are to me. Friends don't veto friends' research proposals. Or read friends' internal mail."

"Alright," said Parker. "Alright. I tried. Don't say I didn't try."

"Nice catching up," said Daisy. "Let's do it again in a decade or so."

Daisy watched him leave.

When she was sure he was out of sight, she went back to scanning the crowd.

Somewhere here, somebody else didn't belong.

She would find them. She was waiting.

• • •

By one in the morning, the ball had taken on that manic edge every party develops when people have accepted that it's going to hurt tomorrow and only care about delaying the pain as long as possible. Even the hired entertainers, dressed up in janky rags and ooga-booga tribal outfits, circulating among the undergraduates in their tuxes and ballgowns, were getting sloppy. One of them even dropped a tray of little blue pills.

Fidget and Nina saw it happen and rushed in to clear up the mess, sweeping most of it into the padded pockets sewn into their costumes. They were here, after all, to steal as much as they could.

Alex watched them move, wondering what it would be like to move like that, with such bold, casual grace.

Maybe you had to be born an artist. He fumbled for a cigarette.

A sharp suck and a slow burn at the back of his throat. A rush of smoke cooled from the lungs, slow-trickled over the teeth, the scrag of rolled tobacco scraps in the mouth and this is the way the world ends—not with a bang but a bonfire.

Nina was suddenly behind him, winding her arms around him, sweet and fast. Her pockets already packed with pills.

"When are we distributing all these, again?" Alex brought his mouth down to Nina's level so he could murmur in her ear.

She just giggled. "Need to know," she said.

"You never tell me anything anymore." Alex squeezed her arm. "I'm starting to think you've gone off me."

"Never-not-ever."

"Or maybe you think I'm police."

Alex said it casually, teasing her. Teasing himself. Made it a joke, deflecting her attention. And it wasn't precisely a lie—he wasn't police; the company employed him to spy on activists. In three years doing this job, he was sure Nina hadn't suspected a thing.

Alex wasn't a bad person. He spent a significant amount of time feeling horrible about the whole thing. Especially since he'd got truly fond of them all. Especially since he and Nina had become a thing.

The problem was, love turned out to be the perfect cover. A white-hot thread of emotion was strung between them, and he spooled it out and pulled it tight, careful not to let it slacken. He did this daily, diligently, with the practice of a professional, and the fact that he really did love her too only made the act more convincing.

He hadn't expected to fall in love, doing this job. Sex, yes, that was understood and even encouraged as part of his cover. A tacitly understood perk. Forge strong relationships, his supervisor had told him after he was seconded to the company. Translation: fuck whoever you like. But Nina—Nina was different. Some girls you fucked, and some girls you married, and some girls were different from all the others. You'd find one of them in a lifetime, maybe, if you were lucky.

Nina was a wonder. A dream in the shape of a girl.

He wasn't going to let go of her.

A breath, a beat. The music stopped.

Then the applause, the whooping of undergraduates who had been drinking since noon.

Alex and Nina swayed together, watching the debutantes dance.

"It's different for them," said Nina, after a while, "these kids. They'll never have what we have."

"What do you mean?"

"Think about it. You only have a few years to be young, and you're spending them with me. Isn't that marvelous?" She took both his hands and spun in them, wrapping herself in his arms. The feel of her small, tight body warm against him.

"You don't ever feel like we deserve another decade or two?"

"Everyone deserves it," said Nina. "But I don't want it until everyone gets it."

Alex palmed a couple of pills from his pocket. Little blue jewels. He held one up to the hollow of her throat.

"Look," he said, "I stole you a diamond." He lifted it to her lips.

"Don't eat the fairy food," she said, smiling a smile that didn't reach her eyes. She was trying to be cute, but it was still a warning.

"Nobody would know."

"I'd know," she said, swatting his hand away. "Be serious."

Alex was being serious. When Nina furrowed her brow in annoyance, which she did often, the lines took a few seconds to disappear. That was new. Pretty soon, she wouldn't be his girl anymore. She'd still be his, but she wouldn't be a girl. He wished that didn't matter, but it did.

"I'm cross with you now," said Nina. "You'll have to kiss it away."

So, he kissed her. She tasted of champagne and hormones; the taut firm weight of her in his hands as he dipped her back, putting on a show for the drunk undergraduates. A smattering of applause.

"See?" she whispered into his mouth. "They won't remember tonight. We will. When you have less time, all of this matters more."

But Alex knew it mattered less.

Nina disappeared to charm some more fix from the fountain-stands. Alex watched her go, the roll and bounce of her walk, and thought, without guilt, of his wife. Ex-wife in all but name. Helen had asked for a divorce three years before. After he took this job. After it became clear that the undercover work was going to be long-term.

"You don't belong here."

Alex turned around as slowly as he could without acknowledging the statement.

"I'm right, aren't I? You don't belong here."

The speaker was a little girl in a dress that she was not so much wearing as occupying under protest. Her bony arms and legs poked out of a confection of pink frills and expensive lace that neither fit nor suited her, and despite the copious champagne on offer, the girl was swigging what looked like neat whisky, swirling in a small tumbler. A slick of lipstick threw her scowl into sharp relief. She looked like an angry macaron.

"I'm with the entertainment," said Alex. "My pass—"

"Got lost, right?"

The girl laughed and pulled a lanyard from somewhere in her frills. The TeamThreeHundred logo winked on the all-access pass, blue and green and sickly.

"I saw the guest list," said the girl. "You and your friends aren't on it. That makes you the most interesting thing at this otherwise boring, shitty party."

Alex said nothing. He made fists to stop his hands darting to the pouch of pills in the folds of his own outfit.

"We'll do a deal," said the girl. "You tell me why you're really here, and I won't call security right now."

"That's really not going to work out well for you," said Alex. Whoever this girl was, she had enough access to see the guest list but not enough to know that the company employed freelance undercovers.

"Oh, yes? Why's that?"

Just as Alex opened his mouth, he felt Nina slip a hand into the crook of his elbow.

"Is there a problem?" said Nina, putting on the sweet-and-probably-a-bit-stupid smile she reserved for authority figures who got between her and a clean getaway. "We're with the entertainment."

Alex groaned inwardly. Nina's sweet-and-stupid-smile trick worked on everyone except other young women.

"Please," said the girl, "let's not patronize each other. I have a proposal you're going to want to hear."

Nina dropped the smile like a hot dish.

"Do we have a choice?" she said. All business now.

"Oh, yes," said the girl. "You can choose to help me have a less boring evening, or you can choose to explain to college security and to my employers why you invaded this party, because it wasn't for the free booze."

The girl sat down and patted the wall beside her. When Nina sat down, the girl nodded and knocked back the rest of her whisky, and tossed away the tumbler. It shattered on the flagstones with a satisfying crash.

"Aren't you too young to drink?" said Alex.

The girl pinned him with a look that made Alex think of dissection tables. "I'm ninety-eight years old," she said.

Alex stared.

"That's not possible," he said, doing the calculations in his head.

"The first fix only got FDA approval seventy-six years ago," said Nina.

"I know," said the girl, "I helped write the patent. You've got some pretty specific knowledge for a hired stripper."

"That's a bit sexist."

"The world is a bit sexist. I'm Daisy. Professor Daisy Craver, currently for TeamThreeHundred."

She held out a skinny, nail-bitten hand. Nina shook it carefully, like a package that might explode.

"And what should I call you?"

Nina shook her head. "Call security, if you're going to," she said.

"No, I don't think I will. Not yet. Nice outfit, by the way," said the girl.

"Thanks," said Nina. "I like yours."

"Don't lie. Liars are boring," said the girl. "Tell me what you're stealing the product for and I won't tell on you. Black market?"

"No."

"Personal use?"

Alex moistened his lips. It had not failed to occur to him that the pills Nina was carrying could, in theory, give them both an extra three years if they rationed them all for themselves.

"No."

"Now, that is interesting," said Daisy. "What would you say if I told you I could get you as much as you want, without you having to sneak around in a bikini?"

"I'd assume you were wired to the teeth."

"You'd regret it. Now, security will get wind of you soon, so I suggest you and your furry friends clear off sharpish. If you want to hear more, meet me in three days at Rose Hill Cemetery. Come alone, no backup, and so will I."

The girl had clearly practiced that part of the speech. She fired it off all at once.

Alex was intrigued. His contacts would be intrigued too.

"We'll meet you," he said. "Where?"

"Can I have a cigarette before you go?" asked Daisy.

Smoking was an affectation shared almost exclusively by fixers and dirt-poor anti-gerontocracy activists with nihilist leanings. Fixers and wannabe fixers because it didn't hurt them and was therefore a way of showing off. Nihilists because fuck it, weren't they all going to die young anyway?

But Daisy Craver smoked in a different way. The same way Alex remembered his mother smoking after she got her final diagnosis. Sucking down each cigarette like it was her first and last.

She exhaled slowly through her nose.

"Fuck," she said. "That's delicious. Alright, go now. Rose Hill Cemetery, in three days. Bring bags like you're foraging. If there's anyone with me, keep walking. Now run away."

They ran. Margo and Fidget saw them and ran too. The tall, thick grass of the deer park snatched at their limbs, like when you try to run away from a nameless enemy in a nightmare.

Alex would have a lot to report next time he saw Parker.

• • •

Letter from Holloway Prison, December 2098

Dear Daisy,

I live in a windowless cell, eight feet wide by ten. I am allowed out once a day to exercise, which means a slow shuffle around a cobbled yard. I speak to the guards, and occasionally to my visitors. By these lights I am not in solitary confinement—I am, however, largely alone. I find that solitude does not disturb me.

There is a mirror in my cell. I don't know if there's someone watching on the other side. Perhaps they have put it there so that I can see, every day, what has become of my face. I thank them for that. This is the face I was always meant to have, my true face. When I was beautiful, nobody thought of my words as worth considering. Not even me myself.

This face makes me invisible, and invisibility is its

own power. I am an invisible woman locked away in a box of forgetting, scrubbed out by a world that still reaches me in hateful whispers—witch, bitch, murderer, monster.

And yet I am freer now than I have been for so many years. Free to tell you the truth of it. And here it is.

The truth is that life extension itself is not sinful. The only sin is to treat time as a privilege. We have been given the gift of extra time to live, to love, to do the work of our hearts. We discovered the fountain of youth, and then we put it behind high walls and poisoned its promise.

I believed this when I was young. I believe it still, now that I am old. This betrayal of the promise of technology is a betrayal of all humanity, rich and poor, male and female and everyone else, too. It is a betrayal as profound as the betrayal of a lover, making the memory of sweetness a sacrilege.

Anyway, I was halfway through the story of the Devil's bridge. Where did we leave it?

The Devil makes his offer, to magic up this brilliant bridge for the carpenter who just wants to get to the other side with his girl, and the carpenter isn't entirely a fool, so he asks—

What will it cost me?

Nothing at all, says the Devil. This is a win-win situation. I will simply wait for the first soul that crosses the bridge, and carry them off with me to hell.

The carpenter is an ordinary chap who works hard and loves his wife. He isn't a bad man, but he makes a bad choice. There's a difference, although you have to squint to see it.

Sounds good to me, the carpenter says.

The Devil snaps his fingers, and there's a cracking sound as the air expands around a beautiful bridge that was not there before. It is sturdy, it is impressive, it has fancy crenellations without being over the top. It's so lovely that if you passed by, however much of a hurry you were in, you'd simply have to stop what you were doing and go and stand on it, maybe take a picture.

If the carpenter knew what we know, he'd know what happens when you make deals with immortals. He'd know that time is different for them. They get more of it, and that matters. It changes everything about the way they relate to the world. To them, we are swift and fragile creatures, arriving after the party has already been roaring for hours, gone before the carriages arrive and the hostess is rascally drunk.

Don't eat the fairy food. Don't make deals with demons. They play under the table with cards you *can't see, and they can make you pay forever, and they are always smiling.*

Do you ever regret what you paid?

Write to me, write to me, and tell me that you're not paying it still.

• • •

Time exfoliates the stones of Oxford University in slow circles. Walk down the wide, quiet high street and you'll see it secreting itself in the deep pores of the university, the fairy-tale libraries and perfect emerald lawns of the college quads appearing and disappearing behind oak gates stuffed with discreetly expensive modern security systems, guarded by porters in black outfits that were already old-fashioned a century ago.

Time moves differently at Oxford. It had done ever since Daisy first came there, two generations before. The sandstone crenellations of the Queen's College and University College still glared at each other across the high street as they would do long after they put everyone Daisy loved in the ground.

They had cars that could drive you right to jail and dirigibles that could get you to London in twenty minutes without burning a lick of carbon. Cambridge was entirely underwater, which is what happens when you build an eminent university in the middle of a swamp. People who could afford the treatments lived for a hundred years and more, but Oxford—Oxford changes slow. Oxford is ritual and tradition and sandstone worn by the wind.

More so now, if anything, because they didn't have to replace the dons as often.

Meanwhile, the other city swirls around the university, moving under the skin but never quite touching. Walk a mile in any direction from the grand worn stump of Carfax Tower, as few of the college people do, head off beyond the checkpoints to the inner city rim, and you'll see it face to face. The slums of Cowley and Headington and Blackbird Leys, crawling with disease beyond the checkpoints. Cramped houses and unswept gutters, the plastic shop hoardings and wind-bitten bus stops where kids with pinched faces loiter in packs, trying to look as fearful as they feel. Their parents all work for the colleges, in one way or another. This is where you'll find the kitchen staff, the college cleaners and maintenance crews, the waiters and shop assistants and sex workers and the men who sell arcane bits of offal in the Covered Market. The people whose job it is to fish the drunken undergraduates out of the river and supply the anxious ones with top-of-the-range psychotropics. There was that other Oxford, clinging to the underside of the leviathan university like a swarm of bright sea creatures cleaning and steering a great blind shark, leading to the inevitable question: Who is feeding off whom? Who is predator, and who is prey?

For the professors, this had become a rhetorical question, a matter for deep discourse and endless undergraduate theses to be printed, delivered and filed away in libraries under philosophical inquiry: contemporary, unresolved, forgotten. For everyone else, the answer arrived each week with a paycheck, if you were lucky.

Daisy rarely came out here these days, and certainly not to the top of Headington Hill. The cemetery wall dragged at her utility overalls as she hauled herself up beside the others. From the top, they could see the whole university spread out like a picnic blanket of rare treats.

Sandstone spires and domes made suggestive gestures at the dawn. Chill mist coiled away from the graves and cupped their faces in its hands.

"It's beautiful," the one called Fidget said behind her—a small, dark young trans man with neat cornrows and clothes that fit like they'd been tailored. Daisy hadn't done anything like this in years—was still unsure if she was only daring herself out of boredom.

She would know as soon as they opened the grave.

Rose Hill Cemetery was where wealthy graduates and faculty members were buried. There was a fresh grave fifty feet away, damp earth tossed before a headstone that managed to be both enormous and tasteful at once.

The rich didn't die like everyone else anymore, but when they did, they did it in style.

"There," said Daisy. "That's where we dig."

Margo, the large, gruff one, rounded on Daisy. "Not okay, little miss. Not at all okay. You said you were here to show us something. You didn't mention grave robbing."

"If I had, you wouldn't have come."

"Not the point. Extremely far from the point."

"It's up to you, of course," said Daisy, keeping her voice steady. Margo was clearly the leader they pretended not to have, the one to convince and impress. "But what's in that hole is going to change your life, and the lives of everyone you know, for the better."

"I don't like this one bit," said Alex, the boring, handsome one attached to Nina. Daisy wondered if he had become an activist so he could pretend he was in an old adventure movie and come out with lines like that. Any second now, he was going to say that it was quiet—too quiet.

"You're secure for at least an hour," said Daisy. "Nobody knows you're here. Trust me."

Margo thought about it. Then she nodded.

"If you're going to be stupid, I'll stand watch," said Alex.

"No," said Daisy. "You won't. Everyone digs, including me. You're all in this."

The soil was fresh, and they got to the coffin within minutes. Daisy kicked the lid aside with care but without ceremony.

The corpse was young, male, fresh. Daisy heard someone, possibly Fidget, make a strangled sound.

Something was growing on the dead boy's face.

Something gray-green and florid and faintly luminescent. His cheeks were veined cheese marbled with furry fungus.

"*Aspergillus aevitas*," said Daisy. "The fungus that's the raw material for the fix. A strain of it, anyway. It grows on the bodies of fixers after death, unless there are extraneous drugs or corroding viruses in the system. Hard to get a control sample. Most of the suicides are overdoses. This kid drowned himself."

Daisy spat out her words like grape seeds into a napkin, swallowing the emotion.

"I heard about that," said the pretty girl, the one called Nina, peering down at the dead boy. Daisy got the impression that this girl at least had seen dead bodies before. "I read it on the local feed. Didn't he throw himself in the Isis?"

"That's right. Poor kid," said Daisy. "Some of them work themselves beyond reason over finals. Need the good results to pay down family debts. Or to prove themselves to the extension-by-merit board. This kid, I don't know. He wasn't one of mine."

Alex made a surprised face.

"One of my *students*," Daisy clarified. "I don't have kids. Not anymore, anyway."

She pulled on some sterile gloves and began scraping samples of the fungus into jellied culture trays. She pocketed a few, passed the rest over.

"We're violating sixteen international patent treaties just by holding these samples outside a lab," said Daisy.

Boring Alex dropped his tray with a yelp, as if it were red-hot. Daisy glared at him, and so did Nina. He picked it up again and put it in his pocket.

Nina cleared her throat. "Daisy has been liberating papers," she said. "She thinks it's possible to develop and culture a generic version of the fix direct from the fungus. Rougher, but it'll do. She needs space and support."

Alex stared at her.

They all did.

"Good grief. That's huge," said Fidget, eventually.

"Are we up for it?" asked Margo.

They all nodded.

"I'll leave by the front gate," said Daisy. "I'll be in touch when I can. I can't stop them picking me up, but I won't get anything more than a smack on the wrist. I'm their weird little pet. You get away out the back. They don't know you're here. They only know I'm here."

"I like the way she thinks," said Margo. "This could be the start of a beautiful friendship."

"Does anyone think it's a bit too quiet?" said Alex.

A scream from the road. The dying-robot scream of a police siren.

"Run," said Daisy, quite calmly. "All of you, run away now. I'll find you."

Nina did not hesitate. She ran. She had made it halfway up the wall by the time Alex caught up to her.

Daisy waited until she heard them hit the grass on the other side. Then she opened a flask of coffee and strolled out the front gate, fixing on her best don't-fuck-with-me scowl even though she was in a better mood than she had been in ages. Sometimes, being a rich man's pet eccentric worked to your advantage.

Daisy had been working that one for years.

• • •

Alex didn't feel like a cunt one hundred percent of the time. Certainly, he hadn't at the beginning. It was a job, and a good one, too, and after his mum and sister died, he had needed any work at all. When the company made their offer, it seemed—appropriate.

Everyone Alex had ever known had died too young, although he struggled to think of anyone of whom you could definitely, absolutely say, "That was old enough." All death was untimely. If that was changing, he wanted in.

It started out with an ad for plain old drug trials, literally bleeding for pay in small hot rooms where they gave you a cup of tea and a biscuit and fifty euros under the table. Then there were the psychiatric trials. They were testing a new anxiety treatment, and Alex had fit the bill: under thirty, in good health, poor and desperate and wracked with daily dread that shook him awake every night with the sound of his own heart shaking the walls of his chest.

The treatment didn't help, but the job they offered him did, after he was found to have a gift for manipulating the truth in situations of extreme stress. Work filled the fearful hours. And then, of course, there was the benefits package.

Alex was a survivor. Alex wanted the fix, and that was the deal, the box of Turkish delight to sweeten the work of professional betrayal: half a century. Standard offer to all TeamThreeHundred employees with security clearance. Shit pay and long hours, but what did that matter when at the end of it all, you got fifty more years, at least?

It was the perk to end all perks.

And all it took was the daily understanding that you were lying to the only people who'd ever actually liked you.

They all lived together in a beaten-up old house at the arse end of Cowley. Alex, Nina, Fidget, Margo, Jasper and a rotating cast of crust punks and lost kids whose names Alex wouldn't have been able to remember if it hadn't been his job to remember their names.

They were all artists in one way or another, and some of them had known each other since school. Margo was a filmmaker who had trained as a state therapist. She was working on a series of documentaries about how mandatory psychoanalysis made people sicker and it would be much better to just give them money. Jasper made clothes out of reclaimed material and bits of scrap metal, and he and Fidget had a comedy sketch show together that went out whenever Jasper's manic moods coincided with the equipment working. Fidget also painted murals, huge angry gray-black things scratched into the plaster-board by an emotion far larger and more terrible than Fidget's small, neat body could contain. The walls were covered, apart from some places where he'd gone right over the peeling posters that had later fallen down, leaving off-white stamps in the chaos, windows opening to nothing, flickering under the LED lights that failed to make much of a dent in the gloom.

Nina wrote prose poems and song lyrics. Some of them were about the tyranny of science over nature, and some of them were pornographic, and some were both.

She had even had a book of them published by a small press that used to run out of the basement of a nearby house before the structure rotted and the tenants had to leave. But she hadn't written for a while and was shy to publish. Alex played bass guitar in a band that had never recorded an album. Then there were the various friends, friends of friends, waifs and strays and lovers and second cousins trying to dry out from drugs, who always seemed to be littered around the sofas and the floor mattresses in the basement.

Making art was a decent excuse for breathing.

Making good art was one of very few ways to earn an honest living.

Make great art and you can cheat death.

They had found each other by chance, through friends and online listings, and pooled their money to long-lease the house. An art colony, like they used to have in the 1920s and the 1970s and the 2040s. It was an end-of-row 1960s pile so dilapidated that it was held together by mold spores and plywood supports. Three out of the five front windows were boarded up, and the garden was full of the corpses of small robots that Fidget, Margo and Jasper had made two years before and tried to train to recognize human emotions. It hadn't worked.

It had all been an adventure for the first year, or two or three, even when there was too little to eat and not enough money to heat the house, no matter how many extra jobs everyone worked when they could. Then, at some point, it stopped being fun. There was more communal drinking than communal cooking, and someone stole someone else's boyfriend, and it all could have gone horribly wrong if they hadn't become political.

It started with simple flyers, just bits of bright cut-and-paste propaganda signifying little. Then it was impromptu bits of street theater. The comedy show got more radical and had to be rehosted somewhere it wouldn't be blocked for extremist content. That was around the time Alex had showed up, running into Nina as if by accident at a housing protest where they'd all been rounded up and spent a cold night together at the local precinct, shivering and encouraging one another to give no information, whatever they were offered. The next night, they were all let out together and ended up in the pub.

It didn't take long for them to come up with the idea of the truck. It was an ancient kebab van with the word "Hasan's" still printed on one side, abandoned in the junkyard at the end of Iffley Road, and as soon as they saw it, it felt like fate. Hasan was Nina's surname.

They paid for the truck out of what was left in the house kitty—the junkyard owner had been glad to get rid of it—and stashed it in the front garden with its nicotine-tipped grass, but Alex was the one with the real skills to fix it up. He worked for weeks that summer, sweat shining off his close-cropped skull, until it was finished. Until it was perfect.

A truck that had been the scene of so many late-night student romances, so many chance meetings over hot chips and curry sauce. By September, Hasan's food truck rode again, under new management, offering one option, mystery stew in sandwich bread, at one, extremely competitive price—free.

It was Margo's idea to take Daisy out on the truck. A test, to see if she was really on board, plus they needed an extra pair of hands to cope with the lunch rush. The engine was so old, it still ran on diesel, and it was always a struggle getting hold of it, especially with the carbon tax so high. But there was enough to drive it to the market every Wednesday and Saturday.

Daisy's head swam with noise and the stink of cooking oil and cheap sugar as she stirred the stewpot. Half of it was reclaimed food rescued from skips—not strictly legal, but not the sort of thing the police paid much attention to, either, unless they were feeling particularly vindictive.

Nina cooked, her long brown hands fluttering over the packets of herbs and bottles of spice. Somehow, she could take any collection of stale, leftover ingredients and suspicious cans of vegetables and turn them into something exquisite, hearty and hot and fragrant, as long as you did not mind that it always came out as a vaguely brown slop with the consistency of fresh vomit.

It tasted fine, though, especially with toasted bread, and there was always a queue of local families, squatters and punks and drifters, lining up for the sandwiches with their mystery grains and multicolored sauces.

And then there was the secret ingredient. At the bottom of each sandwich, smeared with pungent, good-smelling sauce and wrapped in silver foil, a little blue pill, or even two or three.

No second helpings, no money exchanged, no questions asked.

Cheating death was an art, like everything else.

They did it incredibly well.

It was magnificently illegal to resell patented pharmaceuticals on the street, but there was no law against giving them away. There was a donation bucket to cover the cost of running the heaters plus whatever extra ingredients Nina simply had to have to make that day's mystery stew taste so curiously good. Preserved lemon peel. Garlic flakes. Black onion seeds that popped and crackled in the hot oil, filling the rusty little truck with strange perfume.

They worked for eight hours, and Daisy barely said a

word. She just watched the line of people in their dingy clothes shuffle past until the blur of their faces resolved and focused into personhood.

"Do you get it now?" asked Margo as they cleared up.

"Yes," said Daisy. "I think I do."

"As a therapist," said Margo, "I'd say you're making progress."

Then they went home.

• • •

The house was surrounded by sandbags and floods every September no matter what they did. That's why they had it so cheap. There was a crawling-rot stink that no amount of lavender incense could hide, and black mold was always inching its way up the walls because of the damp, leaving everyone with constant allergies and chest infections.

A lot of the house budget went on knockoff medicine. This was the sort of minor patent infringement that Alex should really have been reporting, but he didn't. What with the damp and the drains, they all needed it.

Especially Daisy, who wasn't used to these sorts of conditions.

Alex didn't remember the exact moment when Daisy became part of the household. They had made her a small laboratory in the shed. Easier to do this work away from cameras, away from techs watching your every move and science as a dry dead thing under glass. After a few weeks, she would work through the nights and be there in the mornings, making coffee in her meticulous way in the huge kettle. She'd sleep for a few hours in her chair, eat some jam with a spoon and then go right back to the shed in the garden, where she'd set up a small sterile workspace with some help from Margo.

She was working on her generic, and Alex knew she must be getting somewhere, because Daisy didn't talk to anyone about it, didn't even let anyone in.

One morning, Alex came down to head to the job center, which he still had to do to keep up the impression of not having a job. Parker would hand him a clean, crisp packet of pound notes every time they met—not much, but enough to make Alex feel dirty inside. It was always better to get to the center before the lines started forming around the corner at six or seven, so it was barely light when Alex found Daisy fallen asleep on the sofa.

Daisy sighed in her sleep, rhythmic little whale noises. Alex wondered what you'd dream about if you'd lived that long. Already at twenty-eight, he was beginning to be amazed by the accretion of memory, time building up in drifts behind your eyelids.

Alex was already in the kitchen when Margo came in, rubbing her eyes. She was the sort of woman that Alex normally found intimidating, all short hair and biceps and easy laughter. She could be one of the boys, but she was too much woman, with her broad hips and way of engaging you in conversation about menstrual cycles no matter the hour or whether or not you were eating a sandwich. But she liked Alex, and Alex had always been a sucker for a woman who actually liked him as a person.

Scratch that, for anyone who liked him as a person.

Margo coughed and cursed. "The walls are trying to have sex with my face again," she announced. "This is in no way consensual."

Alex laughed, like he was supposed to, just as Nina came in.

"Right," said Margo. "House meeting time, then. I'll get the kettle on."

"Don't wanna have a house meeting," said Nina, slithering into place behind the table. "I've met the house. The house is a bastard and it's trying to kill us."

"We haven't had a house meeting in two months. It's important to keep things running."

Fidget was the last down. Everyone went a little quiet when he shuffled in, taking his time making tea.

Fidget was Fidget's real, legal name and always had been—he hadn't had to change it when he came out as a boy. His parents were hippies and so was he, albeit in a sensible way he never liked to make a fuss about. He dressed like a programmer and only occasionally invoked the help of his personal muse to beat the next level in *Halo 17*.

He was also the subject of the meeting.

"We're not saying you can't," said Nina, "I'm saying you really should have cleared it with us."

"*I'm* saying he can't," said Jasper, running a hand through his ratty dreadlocks. "We've got a potentially explosive illegal laboratory here and previous warrants out for two of us, maybe more. We can't just be trooping random posh kids in and out of the house. This is a working political organization."

"It's also our home," said Margo, "and it's a safe space for people to express their sexuality however they want."

Fidget cradled his mug like an egg in his narrow, callused hands and said nothing.

"Exactly," said Jasper, "a safe space. And I for one feel far less than fucking safe when I come down to breakfast and there's a fucking Tory boy in nothing but a pair of silk boxers and a shit-eating grin, helping himself to my coffee."

"His name is Milo," said Fidget, "and if you prefer, we can get a different box of coffee so you don't get contaminated by the queer."

"That," said Jasper, "was a low blow. This isn't the fucking twentieth century; I don't care what you've got in your boxers. I don't care what you do with it. I care if you fuck Tory scum in our fucking house."

Fidget stood up without a word and stalked toward the greenhouse.

Nina called his name and went to fetch him back. Alex watched her leave, feeling the white-hot thread tug under his rib cage.

"Anyway. Item two," said Jasper.

"There was a mouse in the sink yesterday," said Margo. "Just splashing about in there, having a grand old time. That must have been where Margo's nice shampoo's been going."

"Mice don't use shampoo," said Fidget. "They're filthy little beasts."

"Maybe they eat it."

"And how do they get the cap off the bottle? With their dinky little hands?"

"I don't think we should use poison again," said Alex. "Last time, it just made them ill. You could hear them coughing in the walls."

"Daisy, what do you think?" Nina asked.

Daisy looked up in surprise. This was the first time anyone had asked her opinion as part of the house.

"I don't think I can comment, really," she said. "Most of my job used to be finding interesting ways to torture and murder mice. In the lab, I mean. For science."

Fidget dropped the sugar spoon on the table. It made a hollow clank. "Didn't you mind?" he asked.

"Not really," said Daisy. "Most of them are raised specially for that. And they have pretty good lives before they get used in tests."

"How horrible," said Margo, pouring the tea. "Before we get lost in theory, though, we still need to do something to at least discourage the actual mice in our actual house."

"We could just get a cat," said Alex.

"We've got you," said Nina, ruffling his hair.

And suddenly, Daisy saw it.

"I'm going back to the lab," she said, standing up so fast, she knocked over two plates. "Sorry," she said. "I'll clean that up later."

"Are you okay?" asked Margo, looking at her strangely.

"Yes. Yes, I am. I really, really am."

Which was, when you got down to it, almost as good as eureka.

• • •

Magdalen Bridge was narrow and ancient and already bristling with people at five in the morning. Alex stood with Nina and Fidget and Margo and Jasper to one side of the crowd to smoke. Not because they were worried the bridge might collapse again this year, although that was definitely a possibility. They were trying to stay inconspicuous.

"Times like this," said Nina, "you can't even tell who's dying and who isn't." She was right. Red-eyed and shuffling in their hasty morning clothes, trading tumblers of coffee and excited whispers, the crowd all had the same face, as if they were going to their graves together, tired and happy.

Nina slipped her small, hot hand into the crook of Alex's elbow, nuzzling into his hoodie.

Above them, Magdalen College was a great marble hand curling its fingers toward the sky. It was almost dawn.

The crowd echoed with the five AM hush, and Magdalen Bridge groaned over the Isis, just as it had for centuries, just as it would do for centuries. Together, they waited for the May Day chorus.

Time works its insulting wizardry on everything that breathes, fixed or free, but Oxford never changes.

A hush fell over Magdalen Bridge.

Everyone craned up at the bell tower.

Then the music threaded up toward the sky, twenty voices trained all year for this moment, words in a dead language falling hard on the pure and savage drum skin of the mind.

The *Hymnus Eucharisticus* rose to greet the dawn.

Alex lit another cigarette and took a long draw, and the rush set his senses spinning as the song rose higher.

"Who wants coffee?" he said. "My treat."

"Sure," said Nina, "I'll help carry."

"No need," said Alex. "You girls just enjoy the show. I'll be back in five."

Alex disappeared into the crowd.

Parker was waiting for him near the coffee stand, as agreed, munching on a candy apple the size of his head. In his oversized college hoodie, he looked even more like a kid. How old had he been when he started fixing? Eighteen, nineteen? Parker was clearly one of those men who, in normal circumstances, would have been baby-faced until he hit his mid-twenties, with those bright blue eyes and long, long lashes that Alex's mother would have described as "wasted on a boy."

"Happy May Day," said Parker around a mouthful of apple. "Have you got a report for me?"

Alex nodded, slid the tiny chip out from under his fingernail, wincing—it always hurt, digging it out—and palmed it across. A nod was all the thanks he was going to get.

"I need you to do something," said Parker.

"What now?"

"There's a logical conclusion to Craver's research.

We've been watching her private work for some time, and it all points in one direction. Your job is simply to observe, and to let matters progress in that direction."

"You're not concerned about the generic?"

"I'm interested in all aspects of the research."

"This is a serious step up from handing out free fix from a food truck. You don't want to stop them?"

"What I want is not your concern right now."

"You're talking about encouraging them to break the law."

"Don't be melodramatic," said Parker. "Of course we don't want to encourage anyone to break the law. Nobody's going to prison if they don't deserve to."

"You remember what you promised me?" said Alex.

"The terms of your contract are quite clear."

"Yeah, well. I have some extra conditions."

"That won't be possible."

"If you want me to do this for you, take a look."

He handed Parker a scrap of paper no bigger than a chocolate wrapper.

Parker opened it, read it and raised his eyebrows. Then he smiled.

"My, my," he said. "You really have gone native, haven't you?" He put the paper in his pocket. "I'll have to talk to my superior, but I doubt this'll pose a problem. Of course, I'll expect your full cooperation. Regular updates."

"Understood."

"Now, I suggest you get back to your—friends. Here," said Parker.

He handed Alex a three-hundred-euro note.

"For the coffee. Every little helps."

Parker pulled his hoodie back up and closed his eyes against the dawn light.

• • •

Daisy worked like she hadn't worked in years. She remembered to eat when Margo brought her a plate of something, which happened about every four hours. Daisy was used to living on candy and chocolate, anything hermetically sealed and sweet, but here they cooked whatever they could make out of food they rescued from the back of distribution warehouses, padded out with vegetables from the kitchen garden.

It made sense. It all made more sense now.

Cells work together like groups, she wrote, *but groups don't work like machines. People get upset and problems happen but that doesn't mean they're broken. People find a way to compromise and work together, and that's what makes the difference.*

The people here weren't like the people who delivered Daisy's patents. They dealt, in their own way, with stories, which meant they dealt in lies. Justice and its meaning. Money and its machinations. Money and justice are all about whose lies are the strongest. But these stories worked together like a lattice.

Science wasn't like that. Science was a truth constantly updating itself. Science was a story without a moral where terror was the prospect of a final page, a final answer. And now the pages were turning in Daisy's mind, chattering and rustling and drawing her through the dark.

And what Daisy knew now was that she could not make the generic, not in the way they wanted it, not with the materials she had. The base material was insufficient. What she could make was something else. Something orders of magnitude more beautiful and terrible.

The forms of genes had always danced for Daisy. She just had to click her fingers and they twisted into new shapes. She didn't need the lab, not for work like this. She could make do with a basic simulation program on a sixty-year-old PC. She remembered when this model came out, its heft and sleek matte surface designed for easy graphic rendering. It was enough. Enough to update the logic of cellular codependency she'd been working on for so many years.

But behind that logic was another, entirely more dreadful pattern.

Daisy found that once she had the steps worked out and the compounds at hand, she could synthesize the new equation quite easily from the stock she'd requisitioned from the lab, where she was still showing up occasionally. They were used to her coming and going as she pleased.

She made a handful of experimental pills, because—because she could, and because it would solve an immediate problem.

She crushed the new substance into powder, sprinkled it on moldy bread and left it scattered behind the wheezing fridge, where the mice whispered and snickered.

And after a few days, the mice weren't a problem anymore.

She stained the rest of the new compound pink to distinguish it from the generic fix she was still working on, and labeled it NOT FOOD.

Then she went upstairs.

There was something about Alex that made Daisy uncomfortable. It was probably just personal prejudice—over seven decades of dealing with their bullshit, she had found it simplest to mistrust every cocky white guy she met. She had probably missed out on some great friendships in the process, but overall it saved time: cocky and insecure all at once, always needing their egos stroked, blind to their own power, white boys were always going to let you down or fuck you over. And if Daisy was being honest—if she was being truly honest, which she found herself wanting to be more and more since she came there—they scared her. Alex scared her.

That was why she waited till he had gone out to the distribution truck before knocking softly on the bedroom door.

"Come in," called Nina, her husky voice muffled by blankets.

Nina was sprawled on the bed in nothing but knickers and a filthy neon T-shirt. The room pounded with music and smelled of incense and old food and, not unpleasantly, female sweat.

"Everything okay?" she asked.

"Fine, um," said Daisy, searching for somewhere safe to put her gaze. "I need someone to help me move the equipment around in the small lab while I, um, titrate the—are you busy?"

Nina absently scratched her lush armpit hair. She did not look busy. "Sure," she said. She yawned and stretched and the outline of her nipples briefly appeared through the taut T-shirt.

"You'll need to wash," said Daisy, still not looking at Nina.

"The hot water's out again. Will a cold shower do?"

Daisy could have done with a cold shower herself at

that precise moment. "Should be okay," she said, "if you put on fresh clothes and scrub your hands."

"Do we have to start right now?"

"I suppose not."

"Come here, then." Nina patted the bed beside her.

Daisy froze.

"Don't worry. I just want to listen to this song with you. We've hardly talked."

Daisy sat down on the bed and fidgeted in the hissing silence before the song began.

It came in clear and pure over a spare, deep bass line that seemed to strip away your skin layer by layer, right down to the red and angry core. There was something in that incantatory beat that held your broken, bloody parts up to the light.

It made Daisy want to drink and dance.

"It's the Future Executioners," said Nina. "Lars Lafferty sings on this one. He's brilliant. They lost their front man halfway through making the first album, and he just stepped up, even though he can't sing."

His voice was perfect for the piece, a biting, sardonic sing-speech, tremulous and cocksure; no, he couldn't hold a tune in both hands, but somehow it worked, like early Bob Dylan, like Lou Reed with all the veins exposed.

"They're playing Cowley next week," said Nina. "Free

gig. They're completely crowdfunded; they still live on their fans' sofas."

The music came in relentlessly—malevolent pop, catchy as an intimate rash.

"The Future Executioners are all about the effect of the fix on the human spirit," said Nina. She seemed truly excited. "They believe that all art is a confrontation with mortality, and if you take that away or delay it, it cheapens the whole thing. Poisons it. If you're going to be young forever, what's the point of writing a book that outlasts you? Or a poem, or a song?"

"I like it," said Daisy. She thought about it. "But what about all the people who've had thirty extra years to develop their work?"

"Mostly dull rich kids."

"Not all. There are the sponsored kids, the scholarship funds. Some people just don't want to see good art die."

"Good art always dies. That's its nature. Listen to the music."

"What's it about?"

"It's about love. About how love is more powerful than time."

"I don't think that's true."

Daisy put her hands to her mouth as if to cram the words back in.

"What do you mean?"

Nina looked stricken, somehow. As if Daisy had taken a precious heirloom and smashed it on the ground for no reason.

"Forget it. It doesn't matter."

"Please. Did something happen?"

Daisy stood up and left her there on the bed. Left the room without a sound. Went back to the lab to bury the memories in work.

She remembered his hands, even though she couldn't quite remember his face.

Saladin had had long slim hands that fluttered when he spoke, when he got excited. He had been a professor in Daisy's department, such a long, long time ago now, before the institute had become entirely sponsored, like all the others.

Half a century gone now.

They were both working on the fix, and they were both quiet, sad people who would rather stay late in the lab than go out to the bar. They seemed to have the same work patterns: days of breakneck, frantic endeavor followed by periods of blank recuperation and remembering to go to the canteen and eat a damn sandwich as cell colonies divided and results compiled. It was only natural that they should become friends.

Saladin was a man of faith and principle. Like Daisy, he had been uneasy when TeamThreeHundred bought the institute and all its patents, but it was a necessary horror—with so much money diverted to defense, how else were they going to secure funding to push the project forward?

That was the subject of their first conversations over strong black coffee in the canteen. Then they started to talk, shyly, about the books they loved, the music and podcasts. Soon, they were sharing playlists. Then they were sharing misgivings. Saladin had a way of pausing before each sentence, as if he were weighing it gently in his brown-butterfly hands, considering its merits and how it could be improved.

"Biotechnology is neither good nor bad, nor is it neutral," he quoted one day, stirring his coffee delicately with one leg of his spectacles in a way that would have horrified Daisy's mother. "That means that it's not enough to just come up with a miracle. You have to consider how it will be applied. What good is all this," he said, indicating the door to the lab behind them, "if it only benefits those who can afford it?"

None of Daisy's training had encouraged her to think this way. Those questions were for philosophers, not pure scientists like her.

"My wife is an illustrator," Saladin said. Daisy tried to keep her face neutral, unbothered. "It's just as important as what we do—no. That's not right. It's not a competition.

These things, they don't work without each other. The precision, the focus, the testing—we can't do that and think about the implications at the same time. That's why we need artists. People who think in entirely opposite ways, working together. That's how we move forward as a species."

Daisy couldn't always remember what was so special about those conversations. Often, they didn't speak at all, just worked or sat together in silence. That's when you know a person is special to you. When you're comfortable being completely quiet together.

By the time they started fucking, it was too late to avoid making love. And nothing changed in the way they would talk, except that sometimes he would call her *hayati*. My life.

Plenty of people had always told Daisy she was clever. That was the only time Daisy had ever felt beautiful. And special. Like she mattered, the whole of her, and not just her brain.

But when the fix was done, when it came time to stand beside the podium, bathed in the white light of cameras as important men made important speeches, Saladin wasn't there. He couldn't bring himself to associate with selling the product at such a high markup. He started writing internal memos, and some of them had verses from the Koran in them. It was a bad time for that. He quit before he was fired.

The last time she saw him was in a coffee shop on Broad Street in the springtime. The fix was finally approved. Saladin had applied for the lifetime extension, like they were all entitled to, everyone who'd worked on the project, but he had been found ineligible, along with his family.

Something about a security risk. Something about extremist ideas.

His beard was growing in rough and scraggy and he looked underslept as he told her all of this. He told her they could no longer meet, for her own safety.

"What do you mean?" she asked him. "What are you doing?"

"Nothing, *hayatih*," he said, putting his head in his hands. "Don't you see? You don't have to be making bombs to be an extremist these days. You just have to have the wrong thoughts. And now they can make sure we all die out."

Then he told her not to contact him again.

And she listened.

He was the only person Daisy had ever listened to, and that was the only time she regretted it, and by the time she did, it was far too late.

The notice in the paper had been small. Noted biochemist, dead at fifty-seven. Pancreatic cancer. Survived by his wife and two children.

Five miles and fifty years away, Daisy put her head on the table of her makeshift lab and listened to the music, absolutely didn't cry.

• • •

All that summer, they worked together on Daisy's new fix. It consumed them collectively. Constructing the lab, making it as professional as possible with the scraps and tools they had. Finding a way to get the base materials in from Daisy's work up at the university, which turned out to be surprisingly easy once they had located the chemical skip around the back of Jesus College. They left the house for paid work, when any of them found it, and to take the food truck out to the market.

Alex wondered if they were still in art-project territory, or if they were doing straight-up politics now.

"Both," said Margo, "and neither."

It was morning in Cowley, and the market had set up on a scrub of grass that used to be a children's playground, out by the busy main road. They had a hundred and fifty toasted cheese sandwiches to make, plus the extra ingredients. The special ones.

"The thing about art is that it insulates you from consequences," said Margo, scooping garlic mayonnaise out of a tub and slopping it onto the bread. "As a therapist, I always think of art as a way of rehearsing trauma, making the unutterable random injustice of life legible, or at least bearably illegible."

Alex thought that sounded like a clever excuse for not thinking your plans through properly. He handed her a block of cheese.

"But when does the rehearsal end?" Margo continued. She paused to lick the mayonnaise spoon. "I mean," she went on, "when do you start to realize that this work is what you've done with the time you've been given? Whenever it is, you'd better have a reason to tell yourself it mattered."

Margo twisted around to hand a cheese sandwich to the next customer, a harried-looking young woman who nodded thanks and passed it to the small boy at her side. Alex opened his mouth to say something, thought better of it, and shut it again.

"Because look," said Margo. "Protests, when they happen at all, those can be understood. The world doesn't change when a bunch of people march from A to B, although it's always good to get out in the fresh air. Art gets to be something else. It gets to be a provocation. To find the fulcrum of culture and exert pressure. So, yes. This is still art."

"Margo," said Alex, "are you high?"

"I really hope so," said Margo. "I really do. It's the only

way I can deal with humans at all these days."

The harried-looking woman was back, without the kid this time.

"Sorry," said Alex, "one sandwich each."

"Mine's not right," said the woman. "They said I should give it back to you." She leaned across the counter and placed the oozing sandwich, which had a small wet bite out of the top, into Alex's hands.

"Who said so?" he asked, but the woman had already gone.

Margo had turned back to the stove. Alex peeked between the sticky slices of bread.

There was a note inside.

Wednesday at 11. Do nothing. P.

Alex slammed the sandwich shut and tossed it into the trash bag.

"Everything alright, babe?"

Margo touched him on the shoulder, and he jumped. He was breathing hard, and his hands had clenched into fists, ready to fight the empty air. He felt like he was having a heart attack.

"Fine," he said.

"You've gone white. And you're wasting food. What was wrong with that one?"

Margo started to reach into the trash. Alex grabbed at her arm.

"What?"

"Please—can you please just hug me for a second?"

Margo stepped back.

"Hey, hey, hey," she said. "Hey. It's alright. You're fine." She wrapped her big, soft arms around him, not too hard, not too gentle, and he let himself sink into her warm buttery scent, shuffling slightly to turn Margo away from the trash bag.

"Breathe," said Margo, "in, and out. Slower than that. Everything's going to work out alright."

But Alex knew she was wrong.

• • •

Letter from Holloway Prison, January 2099

Dear Daisy, and hello Alex.

They have confiscated most of my paper. I enclose the following without comment.

PRINTOUT FROM AFTER SARKEESIAN: A RADICAL FEMINIST CLOUDCAST, FEBRUARY 2099

In all the fuss about the involvement of undercover agents in the development of the Time Bomb, one detail has been glossed over: the fact that at least one undercover agent, possibly more, had a sexual relationship with women activists in the anti-gerontocracy movement. You can find that juicy detail in the court records, but nobody has called it what it is—yet.

Whatever you think of anti-gerontocracy, there's a word for having a sexual relationship with another human being simply in order to betray their trust.

The word is rape.

State-sponsored rape.

This is an old story. For generations, undercover agents in "democracies" have been encouraged to start sexual relationships with women activists. Some of these relationships lasted for years, leading to marriage and even children. The practice was widely condemned, but never forbidden—officers in the early twenty-first century claimed these "relationships" were necessary for agents to maintain their cover.

Interviews with the agents spin these stories as tragic doomed romances. The women involved describe the experiences as a violation.

We believe them.

We believe the women duped into bed by these agents were subject to the same kind of violation. It is impossible to obtain informed consent from a person you are planning to betray—even for the best of reasons. This logic extends *to the consent of the governed.*

Was it absolutely necessary for this agent to have sex in order to gain information? Surely not. There is a difference between cheating and abuse. This is abuse. Sustained sexual abuse. This is rape. Rape should not be part of anyone's security playbook. Not now, not ever.

You don't have to sympathize with extremists to agree with the idea that undercover officers shouldn't rape them.

Stand up for women. Stand against state-sponsored rape. Stand up for individual agency and collective consent. Sign our petition to bring this issue urgently to the Minister for Women and Equalities.

Comments on this update are closed.

· · ·

It was Wednesday, and Nina woke up all in one go, a jolt of energy bouncing her small body out of bed.

Alex watched her through the razor slit of one eye as she padded over to the laptop, dressed in exactly nothing. Pretending to be asleep was the only lie Alex still felt a hundred percent comfortable with.

He watched Nina. He watched her suck her bottom lip as she checked through the feeds.

Her littleness excited him, gray light through the grubby curtains kissing her miniature curves. He always had to stop himself from absent-mindlessly touching her during meetings, even though he knew he'd get a slap for it.

He loved it when Nina took charge in meetings. He loved it when she took charge, full stop.

Yesterday's meeting was six slow-grinding hours of processing the actual potential of Daisy's work. The plan had been to start producing large quantities of knockoff fix and distributing it at cost or lower throughout Cowley, then farther. Margo had already started hitting up their networks in London. But now the plan had changed. Daisy hadn't made the fix. She'd made something else.

The trouble was that even living under the same roof as a generic fix factory technically made all of them guilty of national and international copyright infringement to the tune of several decades in jail. This was according to Specter, an absurdly attractive young dirtbag who owned nothing he did not steal, who occasionally slept on a bare mattress in the basement and surprised everyone by turning out to have two law degrees. Since he was not planning to pay back the debt he acquired in another life, under another name, Specter had also stolen his education, so that was alright.

Alex understood about the patent, sort of. He understood why everyone was paranoid and anxious, as well as excited and constantly checking the windows. Everyone was expecting a raid at any point, apart from Alex.

Alex was expecting it at a specific moment, later that night.

They'd both be out of the house. He'd saved up to take her to the Pitt Rivers Museum to look at the shrunken heads, and then on a boating trip across Christchurch Meadow Lake. Nina had always wanted to go. He wanted her to have what she wanted.

She was so unbelievably clever. Cleverer than most of the Oxford students he'd met. Clever and kind and beautiful. So beautiful. She was so different from his wife.

If she had the extension, she'd be clever and kind and beautiful forever.

Alex had a plan. He hadn't told her the plan.

When all of this was over, he would be getting his own extension package. That was the deal. And if he couldn't get two, he was going to offer his extension to her.

Parker said it wouldn't be a problem.

It wasn't just for him anymore, any of this.

It was for Nina.

He loved her. He worshipped her. And because of him, she'd get to be young and beautiful forever.

Then she would have to forgive him.

A snatch of grimy sheets and she slid back in beside him. Her skin was smooth and refrigerator-chill against his back.

"Hi, sleepy," she said, insinuating herself against him.

"What do you want?" Alex grinned a dozy grin. She smiled back at him. She had one twisted tooth. It made the rest of her face look even more perfect.

"The usual," Nina said, straddling him. "Total destruction of gerontocratic biopower and the money system. Breakfast. And you." She ruffled his hair. "In that order."

He smiled with just his mouth because he knew it was true.

Then she rolled on top of him and pinned him, kissing lightly along his jawline. He whimpered. He always made the most ridiculous sounds with her. He didn't care.

"Do you want me to take control?" Nina's voice was so, so soft.

"I thought you wanted to get to the museum before the crowds," he murmured. She ran her fingers lightly down his underarms, sending little chilly tendrils of pleasure creeping all over his body.

"We'll have to hurry."

She unsnaked the inner tire tube that nestled under the bed for just this purpose and held him down with her thighs as she bound his wrists.

"Too tight?"

"Perfect. But we do have to go soon."

"Depends how quickly you're planning to make me come."

Her dark hair fell over her face, backlit. She grinned down at him.

"Shall I?"

He nodded, yes yes.

She crawled up his body and settled herself over his face, and everything else disappeared.

He wanted her to clamp her thighs hard around his ears, smother him in the sharp meat scent of her, but his hands were tied—he had to crane his head—she wouldn't risk hurting him seriously. She said the last thing they needed was a dead body to get rid of.

Also, apparently, she loved him.

He'd never done this with anyone else before. Not with his wife. Not with any other girlfriend—mentally he checked himself; she didn't like the word girlfriend, she was his partner. She wanted to be his peer. She was crammed into every sense of him, all he could breathe and and taste and touch—

He wanted to drown in her.

He flattened his tongue and drew it down the split of her. Somewhere far above him, she moaned and it sounded like a shout, and then the shouting was everywhere—

the shouting

was everywhere

and downstairs, things were being smashed and

knocked over—

"Shit shit shit." Nina scrambled out of bed, flinging on clothes and tearing down the stairs two at a time.

Alex twisted against his bonds, blinded by panic.

The rubber snapped free from the headboard, cracking painfully against his wrists, and he pelted downstairs after her. Too early, they had come too early. They wouldn't arrest him, and that might look bad later, but he didn't care.

At the bottom of the stairs, something hit Alex very hard in the stomach. A black flower opened and shut behind his eyes, and his knees gave way.

There was really no need for them to keep kicking.

This was all a horrible misunderstanding.

Alex held onto that certainty as the boots found his ribs, his back, and he curled into a ball with the *Hymnus Eucharisticus* sounding in his ears over the screaming and smashing glass. He tasted his own blood.

They didn't have guns. British police didn't have guns.

They had precision flamethrowers.

They had almost everyone on the ground now. There was blood in Alex's eyes, but he still saw Nina go down under two officers.

And Margo—

Margo was running out of the shed with the contents of Daisy's lab, only a few jars of real evidence, dashing them on the ground underfoot and cackling madly—

"Stop right there!" yelled the nearest officer, muffled through his face mask.

Margo froze. In her hand was a plastic packet marked NOT FOOD, with three small red pills, diamond-shaped, like the fix, except—not. Daisy's new formula. The one she'd been working on. The one Parker wanted more than anything. Margo was smart enough to know that this must be what they'd come for.

"Put out your hands," said the officer, aiming his flamethrower.

"As a therapist," said Margo, staring down the barrel, "I advise you to put that thing down and think about the repercussions of what you're doing. This sort of violence can cause lasting post-traumatic stress. Anxiety attacks, hypertension, you name it. Terrible thing for the family that has to deal with it. Are you married?"

As she talked, Margo was opening the baggie with one hand.

On the ground, Daisy raised her head. "Margo," she said, "don't."

Margo lifted the pills to her mouth to swallow the evidence.

The officer raised his flamethrower and aimed it at Margo's raised hand—

—and fired—

—and missed, an arc of blue flame careering up to the ceiling as Daisy bit down hard on his ankle and Margo hit the ground.

Then Margo started screaming.

Something was happening to her face.

"No, no, no!" Daisy was yelling. "Not those!"

But Margo was twisting, wriggling—withering, it was far too late, and Daisy was howling incoherently, and there was shattering glass and sulfur in the air, and Nina was yelling pigs murderers and Jasper made a wet-meat sound as someone knocked him back to the floor, and Alex couldn't take his eyes off Margo's face, the unspeakable wrongness of it.

Margo wasn't screaming anymore. Margo wasn't moving anymore.

Margo had just aged eighty years in two minutes.

Margo was dead.

. . .

They spent a night in the cells. Just a night. The next day, they were all released without charge. In the end, all the police took was Margo's body, wrapped in clear plastic. Twisted and withered and terribly, terribly wrong.

Even Alex didn't understand, not until three days later, when the chip under his fingernail buzzed, a sudden sharp pain, the primitive signal that meant: come to the bridge.

Alex sat on the wall as instructed, his hood pulled up high. The river was deserted. Just one dockhand on the far bank, working polish into the wood of a set of ancient punts. Alex waved and then immediately felt silly.

The dockhand didn't acknowledge him. He was wearing a bulky bomber jacket stamped with the college crest, really too thick for the weather. He must have been roasting, Alex thought. Margo always complained about having to wear long sleeves in summer. Margo's forearms had been criss-crossed with old scars. Margo's face, writhing and wormlike, changing, dying—

Alex put his head between his knees to stop himself from throwing up into the Isis.

After half an hour, a handsome kid in a college track hoodie sat down next to Alex. It was Parker. He looked every inch the early-morning sports fascist, down to the streamlined earbuds chirping out tinny music.

"What do you want?"

"Sometime this week, we believe a member of the collective is going to propose a plan of action. What I need you to do is to make sure that plan of action is followed."

"What is it?"

"Does it matter?"

"Yes, it fucking does!" Alex realized he was shouting. A startled moorhen exploded across the water. Alex lowered his voice.

"It matters," said Alex. "I don't want anyone else to get hurt."

Parker smiled at Alex. "I find that people have a tendency to get hurt whatever happens," he said. "This way, we hope, fewer of them will. You remember the deal? You remember what you get out of this?"

"The deal," Alex said, "is fucking off." He gave Parker a murder-glance. It would be so easy to shove him into the water.

"Go ahead," said Parker, as if he'd read Alex's mind. "I'll get wet, and you'll get shot."

"By who?"

Parker looked up and waved at the dockhand on the far bank. The dockhand nodded, adjusted his bulky jacket and went back to polishing the rowboat.

The bridge was deserted in the morning, just a few bicycles darting by as the August sunshine prepared to boil the dank dew off the grass by the river.

"This is the last job," said Parker. "After this, we'll bring you in."

The morning was silent except for the whispered whine of Parker's earbuds.

"What are you listening to?" asked Alex. "Is that—"

"The Future Executioners," said Parker. "Really inter-esting stuff. Are you a fan?"

Alex chuckled. "That's my girlfriend's favorite band."

"Well, she has excellent taste. In some things, at least." Parker snapped his fingers and the music died. "Now. Are we clear?"

"Yes."

"Come again?"

"Yes. We're clear."

Alex shouldered his backpack and walked away.

• • •

Letter from Holloway Prison, January 2099

What do we want, Daisy? What did we ever want?

More time.

Of course, we never needed chemical intervention for that. We just need permission to live.

Most of us never get to simply pass time. Instead, we're made to spend it. We spend time, and the value of our seconds and minutes and moments depreciates with every week and month and year that passes. Time broken into billable units, and never enough of them.

In this prison I have an abundance of time.

How much, I can't tell you. I refuse to have any device in this cell that tells time. I hear the shift-change sirens, and that is all.

In the beginning the lights in my cell were constant, and I had no way of knowing if it was night or day. This was designed to disorient me. I found it liberating. They gave me a clock, after the first six months. I levered it off the wall with a folded polyplastic plate and smashed it into shards.

I am old in the world's reckoning, and my joints move stiffly, but I am without the illnesses that wrecked my body in youth; I am tired, and I doze, but when I sleep it seems less time passes.

The aging woman is a special object of horror in this gerontocracy. When I was young and beautiful, it seemed that youth and beauty was all there was of me—that losing them would be a sort of death.

There are those who have argued that the fix is more liberating for women than anyone else, given that we have most to lose—always most to lose—when our bodies age, because when they do, men value us less, and therefore we must be worth less. And who can tell us otherwise now?

The fix has changed the dreams and desires of men in ways our parents could not have guessed, but some things remain the same, hard chips of hatred concretizing in the unswept corners of our hearts.

Understand this, though: when I speak of what men desire, of what a man might do, I am not speaking figuratively, of the wants and capacities of all human creatures, with women sounded silently, unpronounced in that great, all-encompassing "men." No. When I say that men are weak and fearful in the face of time, I am speaking quite specifically. I am speaking about men.

Which reminds me, I still have to tell you the end of that story. The one about the carpenter and the Devil and the bridge.

So the carpenter makes the deal, remember, and the Devil clicks his fingers and there it is, the bridge the carpenter wanted, arching over the river like a spine spasming in pleasure, like you'd blush to look at it, it's so perfect and obscene a piece of architecture.

"Remember," says the Devil, "the first soul over the bridge is mine."

The carpenter remembers. He wants to walk on that bridge so badly he can barely draw breath, but he makes himself sit down on the bank. He settles down to wait for some unsuspecting soul to come by and seal the deal.

The carpenter looks out across the river, and that's when he sees his wife.

She's there, on the far side of the river—his beautiful young wife, screaming. Her hair is on fire; her dress is on fire. She cries out to the carpenter to save her.

So of course, the carpenter leaps up without thinking, and dashes across the Devil's bridge to the far bank. His wife's eyes flash red and she blinks out of sight—she was only an illusion, his real wife is at home, wondering where he's got to.

And she will wonder forever, because that's when the Devil appears to collect the carpenter's soul. What do you imagine he's thinking, just before it happens? Does he think of his wife, waiting by the kitchen door, the dinner spoiling, her fine smooth forehead all creased up with worry? Or does he think only of himself, how stupid he was? Does he think about how much it's going to hurt, forever?

They're turning off the lights. I'm out of time.

· · ·

Nobody could get hold of Margo's mom and dad. Nobody knew what to do. Nobody could stand to be in the house.

There was nowhere else to go, so they went to the pub. There was only one pub on Cowley Road that let you smoke indoors. It was run by a mad old Rastafarian, his grim Scottish wife, and their two unreasonably attractive sons. The owner handled unruly drunks and noisy college boys with a small hacksaw.

Also, there were no microphones. The owner would periodically take a crowbar to the walls, just to make sure.

They started to go there every night and drink until closing and smoke till their throats felt stuffed with rusty nails. Then they'd go home.

Nina and Alex didn't fuck anymore; they just held each other tight-tight, like the bed was a lifeboat bobbing on a dark sea, and eventually they drifted to sleep.

Nina woke before Alex most days. She spent a lot of time in the lab with Daisy. By late afternoon, everyone would be feeling well enough to face the half-mile walk to the pub, and they'd do it all over again.

Rinse. Repeat.

In the end, it was all Lars Lafferty's fault.

Alex woke to find the rest of them crowded around the breakfast table, with Nina sobbing, her face a mess of tears and makeup.

"Fucking traitors," she said, her shoulders shaking. "Scumbags."

"Who?"

"The Future Executioners," said Fidget, quietly. "They've started fixing."

Alex couldn't quite stop himself from laughing.

"It's not fucking funny," said Fidget. "It's a sign. A bad one."

"Really?" said Alex. "With everything that's gone on, this is what you're upset about? It's just a band."

He put a hand on Nina's arm but she started away and flicked on the tablet, her eyes wet and angry. It was a short clip from a newsreel. And there was the lead singer of the Future Executioners, Britain's most up-and-coming avant-garde outfit, recent winners of the Mercury Prize, explaining why he was accepting a TeamThreeHundred genius extension package.

"I'm grateful for the opportunity to develop my music over a longer period of time than I'd originally planned," said Lafferty. He didn't quite meet the eye of the camera as the newscaster explained how the sponsorship gave Lafferty fifty years' supply of the fix. "Not many artists get this sort of opportunity," said Lafferty. When he wasn't singing, his voice was perfectly ordinary. "It's all about the music, after all."

"It's all shit," said Nina. "What are we going to do?"

The next night, Fidget brought someone to the pub.

It was an offensively hot day, and they sat outside with the sun beating down like fists. There were always a few students slumming it in the bar, but this one stood out. Tall and neatly dressed, with a sculptured lick of red-brown hair and the tight, too-perfect skin of a fixer. He was white, like Alex and Jasper and Daisy, but a different kind of white—not the ratty, red-eyed, sick-looking kind. His skin had the sleek pink sheen that comes from small, regular servings of very high-quality food.

"This is Milo," said Fidget. "We can trust him." He glared at Jasper, daring him to say something.

Milo shifted in his seat. "You didn't have to bring me all the way out here," he said. "I think I'm getting scabies just from sitting in this prole shop."

Everyone stared at Milo.

"It's a joke," said Milo. "I'm trying to put you all at ease by being a parody of myself because apparently, it's important that I make an effort."

Everyone stared at Fidget.

"Milo is a messed-up person," said Fidget, "but he's my messed-up person, and he actually does want to be here. He has something to say."

"I wanted to invite you all to Magdalen College's alumni feast," said Milo.

Everyone stared at Milo.

"Do they not teach Latinate words in state schools anymore?" he asked Fidget. "Perhaps you could translate."

"I'm sorry," said Fidget. "He doesn't mean it. I think it's a defense mechanism. He wants to see how awful he can be before everyone he meets refuses to be his friend any-more."

"I'm not friends with anyone fixed," said Jasper. "No offense."

"I'm not fixed," said Milo.

"Milo's parents have somewhat antique ideas about in-heritance," said Fidget. "They're withholding insurance until he changes his wicked ways."

"They what?" Alex looked at Milo. They all did, as if for the first time. His handsome grin stayed fixed, but he was gripping Fidget's hand so tight that his knuckles had be-come white teeth in bloodless gums.

"Mummy and Daddy decided to stop my allowance and cut off my fix until I agree to start wearing skirts and calling myself Melanie again," said Milo.

Alex could see it now. The softness of his throat where the dimple should be, the way he kept his jacket but-toned, even in the hot bar.

Milo produced a pack of black Sobranie cigarettes, the sort that cost half a day's pay for normal people, and tried to light one. His hands were shaking. The lighter snick-ered at him.

"Here," said Fidget. His eyes were soft and sad. He held up a flame.

"My Prometheus," said Milo.

Between them, they explained the plan. The plan that

would give them a way in. A place to release a weapon.' A weapon Daisy had extrapolated from her new fix. The same fix that had killed Margo. A gerontoxin, airborne and fast-acting. Diluted and aerosolized, so it wouldn't kill.

It would just make everyone in the blast zone older, and weaker, and that much closer to dead.

It was monstrous.

And apparently, he was the only one who hadn't been told.

This, surely, wasn't what he was supposed to be encouraging. This was the sort of thing he should be reporting right away.

"I realize it's an escalation," said Nina, "and I realize it's the kind of intervention we've never considered before. But me, I hate this town. I hate these people. I hate the suits and I hate the scholars and I hate the state and I hate the way they take everything from you piece by piece until there's nothing left and I hate it that my friend died and it doesn't even fucking matter." She was staring at her hands. Her voice was flat and a little frightening.

"All I wanted was to make something small and bright and good, something that lasted a little while, a little while longer than I did. All I wanted was to push back against the darkness just a little bit. To live in the cracks in capitalism with the people I care about, just for a little while. But it turns out I can't even have that. And now I just want to burn shit down." She took a sip of water. "But that's just me. Don't know about the rest of you."

Jasper slammed his rum and gingerC on the table, his face weird, hard and excited. "Deeds not words," he said. "Christ, I'm getting my first hard-on in weeks just thinking about it. But I can't sign on for anything that gets innocent people hurt."

"Who in that room is going to be an innocent bystander?" said Alex.

He could see them thinking it through.

All they needed was a push.

"I assume you realize that whoever's in the room will be affected," said Milo, "including you."

"That's appropriate," said Nina. "There should be sacrifice."

"Haven't you—haven't we sacrificed enough already?" said Alex.

"What else is there, Alex?" Nina stood up, her face flushed. "No, tell me. What? What else are we supposed to do? Just give up? Slink off into anxious little corners and tear each other's hearts apart and drink and smoke and screw and die? This doesn't end well, you know, whatever we do. We're already fucked. Pointlessly, monumentally fucked. This way, at least we get to decide what kind of fucked we're going to be."

She was so beautiful when she was angry.

Alex closed his eyes.

"I love you," he said. "And I'm in, if you're in. Whatever happens."

As soon as the meeting was over, he fished out the emergency minitablet from the bottom of his rucksack and sent a message to Parker.

Parker didn't respond for days.

By that time, everyone had volunteered for the stunt. Even Daisy volunteered, which was a surprise—or perhaps it wasn't. She, after all, had had a long time to be young.

"There's a chance it won't affect me as much, given how long I've been fixed," she said. "I should be the one holding the device. The technology is mine. My responsibility."

"Actually," said Nina, "you don't get to make that choice."

Everyone looked at her.

"Everyone's a part of this," she said. "Collective responsibility. And you didn't—no offense, babe, but you didn't love Margo like we did, did you? We'd known her years. You've got no experience doing this sort of thing. You're more useful on the outside. And they know your face."

Daisy argued, but in the end, it was agreed: Alex and Nina would go, with Jasper as backup and Milo to get them into the hall. Alex wasn't going to get left behind, and Milo refused to be part of the plan if Fidget was directly involved.

"You can't just make that decision for him," said Nina. "Weren't you listening? It needs to be about consensus."

"Excuse me," said Milo, "excuse me for not being up to speed with your hippy rules, but last time I checked, you can't do this without me. And if I'm going to prison, I'd prefer to have a boyfriend waiting for me on the other side."

Then, quite unexpectedly, he blushed.

Nobody had heard him use the b-word yet.

Fidget squeezed his hand.

Jasper had to shave his dreadlocks, which he wasn't happy about. Underneath, his head seemed curiously small.

Of all of them, Alex would probably draw the most attention, because he was so very white, and Oxford doesn't change, and most of the white people in the room would be eating dinner, not serving it.

Alex shaved. It didn't help. He brushed his hair into a slick parting. It didn't help. He sent more frantic coded messages to Parker's proxy on the backup tablet and received short, curt reassurances that, more than anything, didn't help.

He didn't beg her not to go. That would have been suspicious. Parker had assured him that they would all be arrested before anyone had a chance to do any actual damage to themselves or anyone else.

Nobody was actually going to get hurt.

But still, Alex found himself waking every morning from nightmares where Nina disintegrated to bone and hair in his arms.

He said nothing. He got ready. He let her prepare.

Head office finally answered his messages after a week of signaling.

It was all arranged.

The police would rush them in the service corridor outside the grand dining hall, away from the guests.

When the time came, he'd be there to stop her. There would be plenty of men there to stop her. Parker had told him. He would just have to trust them.

He could hardly trust himself. Every day, he was fighting the panic attacks. Waking up pinned to the bed like an insect under glass, gasping.

Alex walked. He borrowed Nina's earbuds and took a walk through Cowley. He walked over the bridge toward the university.

Alex walked. It was September, and the students were arriving for another year. Sleek silver vehicles crammed into cobbled streets built too narrow for cars to pass. Young people in their best outfits piled out of them with arms loaded with boxes and bags, waiting to find their rooms, waiting for their parents to leave them to the rest of their lives. A whisper of autumn on the slight city breeze, the dying excitement of the year—so little time left, count the hours on your planner, and so much to learn, so many new tastes and stories and strangers to kiss.

Alex left Broad Street behind and headed toward Carfax Tower. He walked for hours. Holding his breath helped with the panic. He would test himself to see how many steps he could take before his lungs screamed and his head swam, punishing himself.

It was too much.

He would tell her tonight.

The house was dark as Alex climbed the stairs. Quiet, except for the rustling of the mice in the walls. They always came back.

Alex pushed the door to the room and found Nina curled in a ball on the bed.

The room looked like it had been ransacked. Like a small and sudden hurricane had flung everything.

Beside her was the backup tablet, the screen alight, something small and black and awful in its dock.

His fingernail chip. How had he not felt it fall out?

Alex felt his heart drop through his stomach.

"It's true, isn't it?" she said. Her voice was flat. She stared at a space two feet in front of her, hugging her knees.

Alex stood frozen with his hand on the doorknob. He gave the smallest of nods, as if his head were in a vice.

She let out the breath she'd been holding, like the air in the room was poison and she had decided to give up and swallow it down.

He sat next to her on the bed and reached to stroke her shoulder, but she snatched herself away.

"Don't touch me. Don't you dare touch me."

"I love you," he said. "I was going to tell you tonight."

"Bullshit."

"Do the others know?"

"Not yet. Tell me," she said. She took a deep breath. "I want to hear it from you. How it started." She breathed out, slowly, not looking at him. "Three whole years," she said.

So, he told her.

He told her everything. The whole plan. The deal. How he was going to save them both. The time he had bought. The time they were owed.

"We'll both get it," he said. "Both of us, for fifty years, maybe more. Enough time to—don't you see?"

"We were meant to be a team," she said, as if she was

talking to herself. "You and me against the whole damn world."

He had always thought she was beautiful when she was angry. Now he knew that he'd never seen her angry, not like this. A layer of shock collapsing into cold rage, leaving something twisted, wrinkled. Something older. Something ugly.

"How could you ever, ever think that after this, I'd want to—fuck, Alex! Is that even your name?"

"It's my real name. It's someone else's surname."

"But your papers. Your identity chit—"

"Belonged to someone else. A child. Someone who died when he was a baby. It's easy for them to rejig the papers."

"You're disgusting," she said.

He put his hand up to her face, tucked a hair behind her ear. She took his face in both her hands and kissed him, suddenly, with a wild tenderness.

Then she pushed him away.

"Please," said Alex. "Please just promise me you won't go through with it."

"I presume you've told your people the plan."

"I did," he said. "You're going to be arrested as soon as you get into the hall. If they get to you in time. Which I'm not sure they mean to."

"Then we'll be arrested. Maybe we'll take a few of

them with us. Now get out. You want to be out of here before the others get back. Get out and don't ever speak to me again."

"Please," he said. "If it ever meant anything. If there was ever any part of us that meant anything to you. It meant everything to me. Just stay at home tomorrow. Please."

"Get," she said, "out."

Alex got to his feet, shaking. He opened his mouth to say something to her, anything. Then he shut it again, shouldered his backpack, and left the house forever.

• • •

Letter from Holloway Prison, January 2099

Dear Daisy,

This is an extract from a talk by some Serbian philosopher who's apparently a big deal right now. I found it in a magazine they brought me—two months late. I remember you telling me what it was like when the internet was more than just messaging and shopping, when you could find anyone's ideas online, talk to anyone about anything. I still can't really imagine that. Everything good seems to belong to the past, sometimes. Anyway, here it is, without further comment:

If one puts aside for a second the question of strict political morality with the understanding that it is dangerous to do so for more than a second one soon realizes that the Time Bomb is as much a paradigm shift in human violence as the machine gun, the tank or the atom bomb. Few lives are lost in its detonation, except at the center of the blast zone; strictly speaking, no injuries are caused. It is a weapon at once entirely humane and utterly monstrous.

The potential military applications are enormous.

The potential social applications are unthinkable.

• • •

Alex ran, his sneakers smacking the cobbles as he tore around the dark corners of central Oxford.

He had to stop her. He had to stop all of them before they got themselves arrested for no reason.

He pushed past the porter, ignoring the shout, and pelted down the cloisters.

They would be coming in from the front this time. Milo would let them into Magdalen with his Bod-card implant. Nobody was going to be looking twice at a bunch of servers filing up to the Great Hall.

The corridor was cold, and old, and very, very empty.

The Grand Dining Room was a vast red rib cage hung with paintings of grim old white men. The guests were black-robed and ageless and tucking into a trifle of force-grown rhubarb.

The servers lined the walls, smart and trim in black and white, and one of them was Nina, and one was Jasper, and one was Daisy, and Milo was somewhere among the guests.

Where the fuck were the police?

Clear, rhythmic sound. Jasper had stepped forward and was banging a champagne glass with a fork.

"Ladies and gentlemen! Your attention, please!"

Nina was on a chair to one side of the cavernous hall, with Daisy beside her. She was a cherub statue with a silver cigarette lighter in one hand and a ball of atomized gerontoxin in the other. It was a rattan thing the size of a Christmas bauble. It didn't look like much.

"We have a special announcement."

Commotion started to ripple through the guests. Alex saw Milo slide over to the kitchen door on cue, but it was slammed shut, locked from the inside.

"You have taken what was not yours to take. You have put a price on what was not yours to buy. You have taken years, and months, and days. Years of life, from billions of people. You haven't shed any blood, but you're still murderers. You have stolen our years, our months, our days. Our moments to live and love and breathe. And now we're going to steal them back.

"We are taking back your years. Right now."

Someone at the back of the room started yelling as it became clear that this was not part of the entertainment, and then everyone was standing up, and the dons were pushing past one another, and at the back of the room, Milo was flinging himself desperately at the kitchen door, which wasn't supposed to be locked, which was never locked, which someone had locked from the outside.

For a second, Alex was frozen on the spot as the noise built to a frenzy.

Then he turned the other way, back to Nina, grabbed her arm, pleading.

"Nina," he said, "baby. Nina. Please don't do this. It's not too late. We can live together, go somewhere, anywhere you want. Please."

People were screaming now, running for the locked doors. A cacophony of chairs and cutlery hitting the floor. Alex was babbling now, begging her please, please don't, please wait.

Nina's eyes were wide and still and terrible as she listened.

She loosened the hand holding the aerosol, just a little.

She looked right at Alex.

"No," she whispered.

She tried to shake her arm free. Alex held her hard. Then something hit him from behind, and he was falling.

"Fuck you, snitch," said Daisy, dropping the serving spoon. "Go crawl into the wall."

She pointed at a small service hatch set into the far wall by the kitchen. Alex looked at the hatch, and then at Daisy, and then at Nina.

Nina looked away.

Alex flung himself into the metal box. He curled into a ball, slammed the shutter down, holding the edge open with his fingers.

He had to look.

In the knife edge of light under the shutter, he saw Daisy grab the aerosol out of Nina's hand. "Get down, *hayatih*," she said. "Let me take it from here."

Daisy's lighter snickered as she touched it to the device.

"Prometheus," she whispered, and pressed down her thumb.

A pair of ghost wings, impossibly huge, opening.

Alex held his breath.

Great trails of light and silence beat and swept across the room and Nina, getting to her feet, she was the dove, withering.

The Time Bomb folded its wings over the hall, and she was gone.

• • •

Letter from Holloway Prison, February 2099

Dear Daisy,

Do you think it was worth it?

What we did, it was terrible, of course. A monstrous thing. A gorgeous, awful thing. We always knew that. But was it the right terrible thing to do? Did it matter enough? We didn't take the Devil's deal. We didn't cross the bridge. We lit it on fire instead, and look where it got us.

People are setting off time bombs in New York now. In Paris, in Johannesburg. In fucking Cardiff. Terrorism, and nothing else, that's what they call it—pure criminality, floating free of politics into pure, abstract fear, clean and convenient. But what does that mean, when everything else they don't want to think about gets called terrorism, too? Teenagers writing slogans on the walls. Schoolkids reading the wrong books.

People send me hate mail, and I don't read it. I

*know what it'll say. Whore. Murderer. Burn in hell.
Sometimes they send me newspaper clippings, too.
Old-school, and those I do read, because I don't have
much else to read. Mostly they don't upset me.*

*This is one of the only ones that did. Please let me
know if you've spoken to Fidget, if you can. He was
the best of us. I'm not glad about much these days,
but I'm glad he got away.*

DAILY MAIL, SUNDAY 7TH DECEMBER, 2098

- "She was more than our daughter, she was our hope": Heartbreaking words of Gray Tuesday victim's family.
- Heir to the Everlong cosmetics empire was killed in the gruesome attack.
- Her mother Juliet said the tragedy robbed them of their "shining hope."
- Described Melissa as a loving daughter with a "bright future."

Melissa Court-Jennings was just twenty-one when she was caught in the terrorist attacks at Oxford two months ago.

Today her parents spoke at the memorial service for families of victims.

Attractive blonde Mrs. Court-Jennings, 93, could be seen wiping tears from her eyes as she remembered her only child. "She was a kind, gentle girl, so hardworking," she said.

The young student, whose father owns Everlong cosmetics, was standing in the blast radius when antiscience extremists detonated the "Time Bomb," aging her instantly by several decades. Most victims survived, but Melissa died within minutes due to an undiagnosed congenital heart defect.

"She never even had a boyfriend at Oxford," said Mrs. Court-Jennings, who was dressed in a black Prada suit. "She said there'd be time for that after her studies. Thanks to these monsters, she never will."

Her voice shook as she described her feelings about the terrorists who died detonating the Time Bomb. "I'm a forgiving person," she said, "but I hope they're in hell, and I hope they suffer."

• • •

There was too much light in the corridor. Alex felt bleached as he walked down to the visitors' room, an exposed thing, stripped of all of his usual defenses—tablet, watch, wallet, even his belt and shoelaces. It had all been taken from him at the gate. Like every time.

They brought her in with unnecessary ceremony, two guards shuffling on either side as she sat down, slowly and carefully. She placed her withered hands lightly in her lap.

"Thank you," he said. "For making the time."

She laughed, a terrible ancient-lady laugh that shook her small body like a bunch of twigs.

"All I have is time," she said. "And more of it than you."

"Are you threatening me?" Alex asked.

"No. I'm not threatening you. What would I threaten you with?"

Her eyes were polished jewels in settings of old leather.

"Why are you here again?" Nina asked.

"I wanted to see you. To see how you were."

"And how am I?"

Old, he thought. "Alive," he said. "Are they treating you well? Is there anything you need?"

"What," she said, grinning, "are you going to bring a basket of goodies for grandma?"

"You know I'll bring you anything they'll let me bring you."

"Ah," she said, "that's a pity. I was about to ask for some porn. You know what I like."

She ran a dark, unthinkable tongue over her thin lips. Alex clenched his jaw to keep from shuddering.

She saw, and she laughed.

"What?" she said. "Aren't I pretty anymore?"

Alex looked away.

When he looked back, she laughed at him.

"Alex," she said, "I am not going to give you what you want."

"I came to see you."

"You came for forgiveness. You're not going to get it. But it's sweet that you keep coming back. Can you take my mail?"

She slid a small pile of papers across the table. Letters, clippings. "I won't bother to tell you not to read them," she said. "Just get them where they need to go."

He nodded. He slipped them into his briefcase as subtly as he could, with the way his hands were these days.

"Still working for the company, then?" she asked. Her wreck of a smile didn't reach her eyes.

"Freelance," he said.

"Checking up on me?"

"If I said no, would you believe me?"

"Not for a second," said Nina. "Go away now. It hurts me to look at you."

"I'll be back," he said.

"I'm sure you will."

. . .

On Magdalen Bridge, an hour before dawn, Alex waited for someone from the past.

The air was brisk and lovely. Alex opened his hands, slowly. It hurt, just doing that. He was holding open the hatch when the Time Bomb hit. According to his doctors, Alex now had the hands of a ninety-eight-year-old—twisted arthritic stumps, aching constantly.

There was a little nest of blue pills cupped in his palm.

Precious diamonds. Fairy food.

Alex's doctors were very understanding. They couldn't fix his hands, but he still got the full package. A century's supply. More, if he did a bit of extra work on the side.

Alex raised his hand to his face and swallowed three of the pills at once, dry. They snagged and fizzed at the back of his mouth.

A little noise like an engine backing up somewhere far away; a throat clearing behind him.

She was there.

She had come, like she said she would. A handsome middle-aged woman in a leather jacket, her mousy hair cut short. Her skin had cleared up, too. Funny how that happened with time.

"Thanks for coming." Alex extended a hand in greeting, too fast—he couldn't make sudden movements anymore—and winced as pain flowered up his fist.

"Have you got them?"

He took the letters out of his jacket pocket, slowly, carefully. Handed them over, gripping as lightly as possible. She took them without saying anything.

"I didn't want her to do it," Alex said eventually. His voice was a weird high warble that caught in his throat. "They were meant to stop you. We were meant to live for two hundred years, her and me. Nobody was supposed to die."

Daisy shook her head very slowly.

"You still don't get it," she said. "You still don't get that that's the worst part of it. None of it was your decision to make. It was hers. She believed in something. You tried to steal it from her."

"I loved her."

"That's not fucking love."

Creeping rose-gold over the little sandstone bridge. It had collapsed last year under the weight of revelers, but they rebuilt it to look just like the original. For half the money, they could have built a new bridge.

"And what about the other thing?" she asked. "Is it time yet?"

"You're still working on the generic?"

Daisy paused, weighing up what to disclose.

"All my research is gone," she said eventually. "I still can't do anything without a fresh fixer corpse. Uncontaminated."

Alex nodded. He fumbled in his pocket for the new packet of smokes. It took him a long time to open the wrapper.

"Why are you doing this?" Daisy asked him. Not unkindly.

His hands were too shaky to light his cigarette. Daisy did it for him. He held the tip to the flame and took a deep, luscious pull.

It tasted like death.

It made him feel alive.

"Do you remember that story? The one about the Devil's bridge?"

Daisy gave him a slight smile. The corners of her mouth turned up, tugged by invisible strings.

There was still time. Not much of it, but they still had time.

They passed the cigarette between them.

"Have someone check the riverbanks," he said, after a while.

She nodded. She did not say thank you. She did not say good-bye.

When she was gone, Alex put out his cigarette.

It took him a long time to haul himself up to the parapet, and it hurt, his hands full of splinters.

There was no safety rail.

Alex dropped into the dark water of the Isis without taking a breath.

Over the spires of Magdalen, the sun was coming up.

Acknowledgments

As I write, a public inquiry into the misuse of powers by undercover police officers in the United Kingdom is ongoing. It is known that several officers used the identities of deceased children to infiltrate protest groups, and that some deliberately engineered relationships with activists to facilitate their work. While the characters in this story are entirely fictional, thanks are due first and foremost to the brave women who exposed these abusive practices and came forward to tell their stories.

I'd like to thank my Clarion West classmates of 2015 for their support and feedback on the first draft of this story, and to Cory Doctorow for his solid advice. Thank you to my brilliant writing teacher Anne Bernays, to wondrous editors Patrick Nielsen Hayden and Lee Harris for their support, and to my agent, Russell Galen, for his faith in me. To Chris Carrico, who cares about the politics of biotech, for the challenge that inspired this story, and to Dr. Sophia Roosth, for changing the way I think about science and social justice. To my first readers, Jade Hoffman, Meredith Yayanos, Cath Howdle, Sasha Garwood, Roz Kaveney, and Emma Felber. To AB, AJ, JI, and the rest of the reprobates, whose idea it was to break into Magdalen Ball back in the day, and to long-suffering housemates Tim Jackson and Emma Ben Lewis, who let us back into the flat afterwards. Thanks to Neil Gaiman and Amanda Palmer for their hospitality while I was finishing this book. To Katrina Duncan, for all her help with everything. And most of all, thanks to Margaret Killjoy, who kept this story honest.

About the Author

LAURIE PENNY is a contributing editor and columnist for the *New Statesman* and a frequent writer on social justice, pop culture, gender issues, and digital politics for the *Guardian,* the *New Inquiry, Salon,* the *Nation, Vice,* the *New York Times,* and many other publications. Her blog, *Penny Red,* was short-listed for the Orwell Prize in 2010. In 2012, Britain's *Tatler* magazine described her as one of the top "one hundred people who matter." She is the author of four books of nonfiction, including *Unspeakable Things: Sex, Lies, and Revolution* (Bloomsbury 2014).

TOR·COM

**Science fiction. Fantasy. The universe.
And related subjects.**

*

More than just a publisher's website, *Tor.com*
is a venue for **original fiction, comics,** and
discussion of the entire field of SF and fantasy,
in all media and from all sources. Visit our site
today—and join the conversation yourself.